Carole Brown has the ability to transport us to the wonderful town of Appleton, WV. and to make its citizens come to life in our imaginations. What could be better than that?

--Larry Vaughn, author of *A Crash Course in the Bible.*

From the moment Toby finds a ghost in his Appleton antique shop, to a grumpy old man badgering Toby's puzzling friend Amy who outbid him at an auction and stole his dream shop, to a sweet and satisfying wrap up, this fourth book in Brown's series is like coming home to old friends. Cleverly weaving businesses and friends from the previous stories and melding them into a new mystery, Brown makes Appleton a fun place to visit.

--Lisa Lickel, author
the Buried Treasure mysteries
and the upcoming Fancy Cat mysteries
from Prism Books,
an imprint of Pelican Ventures LLC

"I was as delighted with meeting the unique array of characters as I was watching the mystery unfold."

--Cheryl Colwell, suspense author

Carole Brown is a prolific writer who captures the hearts of her readers. Whether she's writing fiction, non-fiction or children's books, you can expect a blessing.

The latest book in the Appleton, WV Romantic Mystery series is a page-turner you can't put down. If you are gifted with that "unique investigative gene" you will be trying to solve the mystery from the first chapter to the last, but you'll never find the answer until Carole reveals it in the last few pages of the book. Sweet romance and intrigue will keep you reading until the mystery is solved.

--Ann Knowles, author, editor, and owner of Write Pathway Editorial Services

Carole Brown writes with a touch of humor, just enough mystery-suspense to keep the reader turning the pages to see what happens next, and a nice mixture of sigh-worthy romance. Looking forward to the next book in the series.

Carol Ann Erhardt, Christian Romantic Suspense author of *Joshua's Hope* and the Havens Creek Series

Carole Brown does a wonderful job of balancing romance and mystery, keeping her readers engaged while at the same time entertained. This series is a good read for anyone who loves curling up with a good book, one that will cement your faith in happy endings.

--Barbara Derksen, author of the Wilton/Strait and Finder Keepers Mystery series

Thanks for reading my book! Carole 7-2018

Toby's Troubles

An Appleton, WV Romantic Mystery

Carole Brown

Story and Logic Media Group
Printed in the USA
... For the discriminating reader
...because we believe story *needs* logic.

Toby's Troubles: © 2018 by Carole Brown
An Appleton, WV Romantic Mystery (4)

 Published by STORY AND LOGIC Media Group ... For the discriminating reader ... Because we believe story *needs* logic.

Cover Design by SAL media
Printed in the USA

ISBN 13: 978-1-941622-60-5
ISBN 10: 1941622607

Library of Congress Cataloging-in-Publication Data
Brown, Carole
Title: /Carole Brown
ISBN 978-1-941622-60-5 (pbk)

1. Series fiction 2. Cozy Mystery 3. Romance
4. Inspirational fiction

1. Title Library of Congress Control Number: 2018949203

Carole Brown

Undiscovered Treasures

Toby's Troubles

An Appleton, WV Romantic Mystery

Dedication:

Daniel Lee, my firstborn son.
I remember all the laughter we've shared,
the conversations where we've talked about
serious and silly things,
the gifts from your loving heart you've shared
with those less fortunate,
the strength you've given to those less strong,
your thoughtfulness to your father and me.

You'll forever be in my heart.
I love you!

And to a sweet, dear person
who is a real friend.
Fun to be with.
Shares many, similar interests with me.
Interesting conversations we've shared.
Talented, devoted, and serious about God.
I love you much!

Acknowledgements

Theresa, so glad we're working together as
critique partners. You've been a life saver to
me.

Michelle, I didn't realize how much I needed
your writing help till this year.
I thank God for your encouragement and edits.

Jon, your help when we discussed a part of
this book was a real break-through for me.
I can't begin to thank you enough for that.
Meant more than you'll ever know.

And, again, Sharon, thank you for being there.
For the push you give me.
For listening.
For being my editor.

Sometime in the past, I heard the advice, that
when writing a book,
and you reach a tough spot, keep writing.
Doesn't matter what; just write.
For this book, that's what I did.
Yeah, it was tough at times.
But there were times of inspiration,
times when the light shone through,
and I knew just how to proceed with the scene.
There were times during this year, when I was
way too busy,
but I kept plugging along.
And I finally made it.
I typed "The End."
Thank you, God, for that!

Chapter One

Present Day

Toby Gibson didn't believe in ghosts.

Or at least he hadn't until recently.

Slowly, he opened his eyes—but just a crack—and shifted his gaze from one side to the other as far as he could see.

Which wasn't far, seeing as it was pitch black in his bedroom. Just the way he liked it. But if he was going to snag the current ghost in his home, he was going to have to forget about getting spooked if he did happen to see it.

He chuckled, sat up, and reached for the flashlight he'd placed on his nightstand just in case the Undiscovered Treasures' ghost decided to show up again. He and his sister, Caroline, had never been bothered with ghosts before here at their antique, collectible, junk shop, so why now?

Flashing his light around the room, he saw nothing unusual. Hmmm. Did that mean it had moved on to a more exciting home?

Not if the faint, faint sounds coming from the first floor were any indications.

Three times before the ghost had deigned to visit. Rustling noises, light bumps and rustlings in the night, disturbances in the shop itself—all these and more gave definitive clues that someone—or something—was entering their business.

Toby swung his legs to the floor and stood,

edging as quietly as he could in his bare feet to the door. He twisted the knob and peered through the crack, but only a dim nightlight illumined the short hallway.

Twice before he'd tried to catch the ghost, but had failed. Maybe the third time would be the charm he needed. Stepping as softly as he could, he headed to the stairs and took one step at a time, making sure to avoid the second from the bottom that squeaked as noisily as a mouse would when caught in a trap by the tail.

At the bottom, Toby drew in a deep breath. The sounds were coming from a side room where he always placed the newest items he'd found and bought so they could be evaluated, inventoried and priced before being placed in the main section of the store.

An unusually loud noise had him mentally perking his ears. What on earth was the thing doing? He'd soon find out.

Tiptoeing, unlit flashlight still in hand, Toby moved toward the room. The door was cracked a hair, and he paused, listening.

A slight scooting sound as if it was pushing a heavy object...or was it a warped drawer opening? Then a faint ruffling sound. Was it sifting through something and allowing it to fall gently back into the container? Rummaging through cloth?

Toby gave the door an easy shove. Across the room, a light shone on an antique cabinet that needed a touch of repair before he and Caroline could sell it. Doors were opening and shutting.

Unlike the regular storage room, this windowless room was so dark, Toby could see nothing but that bit of light shining here and there on the cabinet. He had no idea what the ghost looked like or whether it was a bad ghost or good one.

A chuckle spilled from his throat at the thought, and the ghost whirled, shining the light directly into his eyes, blinding him.

He heard the ghost coming, felt its nearness, the faint scent of something musky and strong drifting in the air. Without pausing to think, Toby lifted and struck out at the thing with his flashlight as it passed him.

A raspy grunt.

The sound of staggering feet.

A growl.

And the thing ran down the hall, ducked into the main selling room. By the sound of it, he/she/it slammed open the front door, and without bothering to shut it, left without a word.

That was pretty callous out of the—well, he was going to say ghost again, but now, having met him in a manner of sorts, he'd have to say—person. The least the fellow could have done was say "Hi," or "Thanks for letting me search your business".

Or explain what he was doing.

Or looking for.

Chapter Two

Two Months Earlier

Toby had never been to this auction house before, but it'd been promoted as an established and lauded place to find and buy unique, and sometimes, valuable items. As an estate auction, they were well known and trusted to get the best possible prices for the heirs.

He eyed the woman ahead of him. Amy Sanderson had clued him in on the place, expressing her intense interest in checking out some of the advertised pieces, and here they were. What she was after, he had no idea, but it was nice to have someone like her along. Unlike Ryle Sadler's usually quiet persona, Amy's chatter was enlivening and fun, meant to keep him on his toes. He edged closer and eyed the set of lamps she seemed particularly fond of.

"Anything in particular you're looking for?" Might as well try to find out what his friend was after.

"One or two things. We'll see, depending on how high the bidding goes. I've set a limit. Beyond that, I'll let it go." Amy winked at him and started to move on.

"It's almost time. Want to grab a seat?"

"Sure. I'm done looking."

In the huge auction room, they chose the last two chairs in the second row, right hand section. He nodded at one or two people he'd talked with at previous auctions, but ignored the majority. They, like he, was only interested in one thing: bidding high enough to obtain that one precious item that would make them money.

Toby had his eye on three or four items he hoped he could get. One was a bedroom chest and bed. Strong and durable, he had a personal interest in it rather than business. He was hoping Toni could get to remodeling his apartment upstairs—unless other plans he had materialized—which would give him the space he wanted to use this bed. Far more comfortable than the twin he now used. When the bidding began for the two, he raised his paddle...and promptly got the shock of his life.

Toby's hand had barely dropped when Amy raised hers, and he turned to stare at her. What was she doing?

Another bid came from behind them, and Toby raised his paddle. Again, Amy raised hers.

For the next three minutes the bidding was fierce. Toby almost forgot there was a third party in his anxiousness to outbid Amy.

It didn't work. Blithely, and with a small grin, she kept raising her paddle until he realized he was way over the price he'd determined was his limit. With a regretful shake of the head, he relinquished the bid to Amy, and the auctioneer blared out her victory.

When the auction was over, Toby turned to Amy. "What were you doing? I wouldn't have bid on that set if I hadn't wanted it."

"I realize that. But I wanted it too."

Toby seldom allowed himself to be angry or

hurt at someone's intentional or unintentional actions, but today...he wasn't sure how he felt. The woman he'd always felt was his friend— maybe close to being a best friend, deliberately setting her mind to outbid him.

"Why did you want the bed?"

She cast him a smug look. "I have very special plans for that bed. Come along. Let's get the payments made. I'd love to check out that new diner Toni was talking about last week."

Without another word—as if she had no sense that he was peeved—she moved toward the cashier, assuming, he supposed, he'd follow.

"Excuse me."

A hand touched his shoulder, and Toby turned.

It was an elderly, distinguished-looking gentleman, his white hair thin, but well groomed, his dark gray suit immaculate. He clutched a cane, slick black with a gold embellished eagle handle. The man was pale— almost sickly—but, nevertheless, carried an air of entitlement about him.

"I'd like a word with you."

"How may I help you?"

"I want to buy that bed set you just bought."

"I didn't buy the bed set."

The man tapped his cane. "I'm sure you did. I will pay a good price."

"You're mistaken. I wanted it, but someone else bid higher. It was..." Toby's voice trailed off as Amy swiveled to look at him and shook her head.

Was she telling him not to reveal who bought it? Or was she confirming that she didn't want to sell? Either way, the man had abruptly swung around enough to catch her gesture. As if he'd brushed Toby off like a piece of lint that dared touch his clothes, he headed toward her.

"Young lady, I want that bed set you bought. I'll pay an excellent price."

"I'm sorry. I can't sell it."

He glared at her. "Why not?"

"I have a reason for buying it. A very good reason."

"Fiddlesticks. That's nonsense. Anything can be bought for the right price."

"Not this."

Her chipper voice did nothing but agitate him even more. His face grew red, and the cane tapped another three times on the marble floor.

"I insist."

Amy's face was a study, and Toby wanted to laugh. "Maybe you should consider it? He seems to really want it, and you know, you don't need it."

"Why would you think that?" If her voice was anything to go on, she was very vexed. And it probably wasn't at the old man.

"But it's much too big for your place..." He grinned at her.

"What makes you think I'm going to use it?"

"What else...?"

"Right. Maybe I have plans for it. My sister could use it, I'm sure. And my parents, though seldom at home, love antiques."

"But he offered an excellent price."

"Not interested."

"Are you two done?" The elderly gentleman

had obviously had enough of their bickering.

The look Amy sent Toby didn't bode well for their later plans.

"Why do you want it?"

"That's none of your concern."

"I'm sorry, but I'm not selling." Amy moved away.

The man sputtered, but Toby's friend paid no attention.

"Can you not persuade her?"

"Me? No, I can't. Or maybe I won't. Either way, it's none of my business. She doesn't want to sell, so I see no option but for you to accept her decision."

"Nonsense." And again, the cane thudded its angry tap. "I always get my way."

Toby walked away and didn't say the words he thought.

Not this time you don't.

Chapter Three

Present Day

"**P**at, have you heard anything more about that property I want?" Toby tucked his cell phone under his chin and flipped through the papers he was working on.

"Can you believe it? There's another bid on the same place."

"Are you kidding me? After all this time?"

"Not kidding. I ran into Finch at lunch time, and he said his client had put in a bid."

"Did he say who it was?"

"No. He wouldn't. These are private bids for the place. I'll give you a heads-up if we have to raise our bid though."

"Thanks, Pat. I can't understand why someone would be bidding on it. It's sat empty and deteriorating for years...and now someone's suddenly interested in it the same time as me?"

"Yeah, crazy. Listen, I've got to go, but I'll be in touch. We still have a good chance. No one's going to bid too high on that place."

"Let's hope not." Toby tapped impatient fingers on the countertop. "I think I'll run over to the property and take another gander around. See if I want to raise my bid higher. I think I offered a pretty good price for the rundown place."

"You did. But seems someone else wants it as much as you do."

"I guess. Talk later."

Toby laid his phone on the countertop and stared at it for a minute. That was strange. The building next to his had sat empty for years, the owner refusing to sell or do anything about inside upkeep and minimal outside work. Taxes were a different story. The owner had paid them regularly and on time. Toby and his real estate agent had been shocked when word had gotten out the man was finally selling.

He had jumped at the chance. The idea had hovered and grown through the years of owning the property and expanding his work. The added enticement of creating a luxury apartment in the upstairs was an added appeal. And it'd give Toni DeLuca-Douglas, one of his sister's best friends, and her inherited construction company a great summer opportunity for work.

Now?

Now it was time to do some detecting as Caroline always loved doing. Too bad she was overseas with her husband.

First things first. As contrary as the owner of the next door building was, and Toby ought to know—he'd known the man since childhood—the man had insisted on Toby keeping a key to occasionally check on the place, being right next door. If a problem developed, he wanted Toby to be able to find and fix it, or, at the least, hire a cheap contractor. And Toby had always been willing—especially since that germ of an idea in the back of his mind expanded, applauding any close association he could get with the place.

He closed his notebook and locked the door. A little early for lunch, but that was okay.

Business was slow today which was normal for a Tuesday. Plenty of time to do some more dreaming...and detecting.

~*~

Grabbing his flashlight, Toby headed next door. What he hoped he'd find, he had no idea. It'd been awhile since he'd checked out the place—even before he'd offered his bid. But it might be better to see if, perchance, the owner had made improvements that impressed a possible random buyer to offer an unexpected bid. Doubtful, but still worthy of a look-over.

Toby walked up the crumbly cement walk but stopped before approaching the door. Off to the side of the walk, up close to the building, were a multitude of footprints pressed deep into the dirt. As far as he could guess, only one person and his/her agent should have been here legally, if what his real estate agent had said this morning was true. Way too many footprints for two people, and besides, why would they be off the sidewalk, walking on the dirt where a long ago flower bed had been?

Checking out the exterior of the building? Maybe.

Toby glanced at the disturbed dirt. That was an awful lot of prints. Maybe they were the restless type. He chuckled at his own foolishness.

He twisted the key in the lock, and Toby shoved open the protesting door. The place was a mess, but that was normal. Dust everywhere, yellowed newspapers here and there, left over items from the printing shop scattered about. But nothing looking any different since the last time he'd checked it out.

He strolled the bottom floor checking out each room. It was a spacious building, still in basic good condition. That was one thing that had attracted him to it. A firm, solid foundation that would need little work, and strong outer walls. The interior was another matter and would require extensive repair, but Toni's construction business could handle that, no problem.

The creak came just as he'd made up his mind to leave. He didn't have to guess or wander around trying to figure where it'd come from. He knew. Halfway up the stairs, a step screeched out its creak.

Toby stared up the stairs but because of the sharp turn midway up, he couldn't see clear to the top. Should he check it out? Could be it was a rat or even a cat. Last time he was in here—a month ago—he'd noticed a broken window, so it would easy for a varmint to enter.

Even a two-legged one.

He hadn't gone three steps when he heard the running footsteps. Slap. Slap. Slap...

Someone was running—but where to? There was only one set of stairs.

Toby sped up the stairs, hit the squeaky step, moved on to the top and stopped. The footsteps had quieted too, but he could almost hear the heavy breathing. Was the ghost— oops!—person waiting on his next move?

He edged against the wall and eased forward. Something slammed, distant footsteps seeped into the hallway, and he ran toward the sound. In the middle room, facing his own property, a window stood open. Hurrying to it, he leaned out and caught a glimpse of a dark head easing off of the porch roof.

Scrambling out the window after the guy, he was just in time to see him jump from the stationary ladder and streak toward the front of the building. Tall and thin, Toby was almost sure the guy was young.

What was he doing inside? By the looks of his clothes, he didn't look homeless. If his shoes were anything to go on, they were expensive and name-brand.

And it looked like—no, couldn't be—someone he knew, someone he liked.

Ryle Sadler.

But that was crazy thinking. Ryle would never attempt such a stupid stunt.

Casting the thought from him, he ran over all the dark-haired men he knew, but nothing stood out.

Why break in? Nosy? Mischievous? Hiding? He'd better have a look around.

Back inside, he turned for another look out the window and realized that he could see straight into his own building from the two, large side windows. One shot was of the front countertop. The other granted the viewer a glimpse into the storage room. Not that it would be an easy view. Most times he kept the blinds shut, but when working in there, he always opened them. In fact, in good weather, he drew them up and opened the window, affording anyone who wanted a nice picture.

Was someone spying on him? Or looking to loot his business?

And did any of this have something to do with the person breaking into his business in the middle of the night?

~*~

Toby was locking up the door to the next door building when someone spoke from behind him.

"Been looking for you. Thought you might have taken the afternoon off. You want me to help out a little today? I'm free this afternoon."

He recognized the voice without turning around. As usual, Ryle showed no curiosity, whether it was from actual noninterest in Toby's doings or an attempt to prevent questions about his own personal life.

"Sure do, Ryle. Would you finish the inventory for that newer batch of items we purchased last week? I'm going to get a head start on our income taxes, I think." He grinned but gave the boy a casual look-over. Shoes, dark like the intruder's, but no hoodie. That didn't mean he hadn't tossed it aside though. "Unless something more interesting interrupts me."

"Not my favorite thing to do by a long shot." Ryle headed back to Undiscovered Treasures. "I'll get started on that inventory."

The earlier suspicion fluttered into his mind like a sinister creature disguised as a beautiful butterfly, and Toby shook his head. He hated that thought. Ryle would no more spy on him than Amy would...

"Boo. What's the most special proprietor in Appleton doing standing outside an empty building instead of working hard at his prosperous enterprise?" Amy peeked from the corner of the building, her laughing eyes twinkled at him.

"The bigger question would be: why aren't

you working?"

Amy walked toward him. "It's much too nice of a day to be inside, so I decided to stroll around for a bit before tackling the orders received this morning."

"I see." Toby eyed Amy's business on the far side of this empty building—Bloomin' Life, the best and only flower shop in town. After Amy had bought it, she'd hired Toni DeLuca-Douglas to remodel it. She'd captured Amy's dream for the place and turned it into one of the most distinguished businesses in town. Large twin windows on either side of the recessed door showcased the owner's newest creations. Subtle lighting both in the windows and inside the main room enticed prospective customers to browse and stay awhile.

And buy.

"You've done well with your business."

Any swiveled to stare at her own building. "Yes, I have. I'm blest to be doing a job I love. I can't wait to fulfill the rest of my dreams."

Tucking her hand within his arm, he tugged, and she followed.

"What would those dreams be? Isn't living here in Appleton enough for any fair maiden?"

"I perceive, my Lord, ye are projecting yourself into one of our fair community plays."

"Nay. Thou art wrong. It shall be 'off with your head.'"

"What fun you and Caroline must have had as children. You're both so unique and fun to be around."

"Any more sweet compliments about me you want to hand out? My feathers have been ruffled."

She put on a shocked expression. "Who would dare?"

"That's just it. I have no clue who's provoking my wrath."

"Sounds serious." The fun vibrating in Amy's voice seconds earlier had disappeared.

"Yeah. Bested by an unknown opponent." He corner-eyed her. "Not really. I'm exaggerating, but it is shocking to know just when I decide to buy this building between us, someone has suddenly developed an interest in it too."

Amy stopped dead. "*You're* really trying to buy that place? I know you talked about it, but I thought you were joking."

"Took me awhile to decide if I wanted to tackle it, but I need the space. My special dream is to create a full-sized living area, and by emptying out all the storage rooms upstairs, and with Toni's carpentry talent, it's a feasible plan. Then I'm considering the possibility of opening my own auction house. The downstairs is big enough, and with just a few minor changes, I think that could be accomplished. My business next door..." Toby nodded at Undiscovered Treasures building. "...would have the upstairs as a bigger office area and a place to keep smaller items in storage till needed."

"Really, Toby? You want to do all that?"

"Yes, I do. But I can't use all my money on outwitting this potential buyer and then come up short for needed repairs."

They walked on, and Amy was silent for a moment.

"And you don't know who this bidder is?"

"Have no clue. Yet."

"Your agent doesn't know?"

"He says he doesn't."

"I know who it is."

"*You* do?"

Her head nodded.

Silence.

"How on earth did you learn this? It's supposed to be a sealed bid auction."

What was going on? Sounded like some shady doings.

"Are you going to tell who it is? Maybe I can talk some sense into this person."

"You mean talk him out of buying the place?"

"Yes."

"I doubt it. From what I understand, they're very interested. I gather they have some elaborate plans of their own."

And she knew this how?

"Are you going to tell me who it is? A friend of ours? Someone I don't know?" As a thought struck him, he stared at her. "Your parents? Does your dad have a business scheme he's working on? If that's the case, I'll never be able to outbid him."

"No, it's not my dad." She smiled, her blue-green eyes twinkling at him again. "Is that your plan to outbid the other person?"

"I might have a go of it. Depends on how high they're willing to bid."

"I see."

"I'm not going to beg you to tell me."

"You're upset at me?"

"No..."

"Good. It's me."

"You what?"

"I'm the one bidding on the building."

Silence. Again. This time it was of his own doing.

Amy? His friend? Going up against him in bidding on this building? How many times had he talked about it with her? It wasn't like she didn't know how much he wanted it.

"You are upset at me."

Her lips parted in another smile, but he wasn't laughing.

"Yes, I do believe I am. Are you doing this to irritate me? Why would you want such a monstrosity? Besides, you've known forever I was considering buying it. If you were interested, why didn't you tell me?"

"I have my reasons. I didn't know you were bidding on it till now."

"Seriously?"

"Seriously."

"Would you have bid on it if you'd known?"

"Maybe. Depends."

"On what?"

"Now that's one question I won't answer right now. Talk to you later."

Maybe you will and maybe you won't.

But he knew he would. His faith forbade him from holding grudges, especially at someone as sweet as Amy.

That didn't mean he had to like what she was doing.

Chapter Four

Two days later

Toby Gibson stood at the doorway of the large storage room of his shop. It was crowded, but not overly so, and at least, organized to a certain degree—thanks to him. His sister was anything but organized, but he loved her in spite of it. She was an ace salesperson though and allowed him to do what he enjoyed: the buying. Worked good for both of them.

Now that she was happily married to his best friend—Andy Carrington—he had the whole upstairs apartment to himself. Felt pretty good actually, on his own for the first time since his parents' freak accident. Both teenagers, it'd been a devastating blow

They'd had to spend three years with their crazy aunt—their mother's sister, before heading off to college. Even though he was almost a year older than Caroline, he'd waited till she finished high school so they could head off to college together. And once they'd graduated, they'd been thrilled to take the money their parents had saved for them and start Undiscovered Treasures. It was up to him now to figure out why they'd had three—no, four—break-ins in the last month. It was getting kind of old.

He gazed at the huge cabinet the would-be thief had searched three nights ago. Surely if there'd been anything more valuable than the cabinet itself, the guy would have found it.

Toby shrugged and headed for that particular piece of furniture.

Forty-five minutes later, after feeling for hidden panels and drawers, using his trusty flashlight to search below the shelves, and loosening the back of the cabinet enough to peer into it, he gave up. Whatever valuable thing he'd accidentally bought at that last auction would remain hidden. He had no clue what or where it could be.

"Toby, are you here? Are you busy?"

Amy Sanderson.

"I'm in here, and I'm always busy."

Seconds later, her dark blond head peered into the storage room. "Why are you in *here* this morning? Thought you did your inventory on Mondays."

"I'm not inventory-ing."

One shapely brow lifted and a small smile lifted the corner of her heart-bud lips. "Then...?"

"The ghost stopped by for a visit again."

"Toby..."

The reproach in her eyes chided him, albeit fondly.

It was too bad no one was taking him seriously. Amidst the laughter and jokes, you'd think he was the biggest "wolf-crier" ever, as in "The Little Boy Who Cried Wolf."

"Just kidding. But someone did. Woke me up around two. Got in a decent clobber at him, though. That was some satisfaction."

"Why am I just now finding out about this visit and why on earth don't you call the police?"

"Why? They'd just waste my time writing down a bunch of information that won't help a bit. Besides, the guy hasn't hurt anything yet."

"You're not taking this seriously. Any legitimate person wouldn't be breaking in. What on earth are they looking for?"

Toby shrugged. "That's what I've been doing for the last hour. Scouring the cabinet he seems obsessed with, but if there's anything valuable in that, I can't find it."

"Want me to take a look?"

Toby studied her. She was the best girl he'd ever dated, and that was a lot. But lately—well, suffice it to say, she'd had that look in her eyes that meant she was thinking serious thoughts. That meant trouble was ahead. Which he didn't need nor want. He liked his freedom just fine, thank you very much.

Why couldn't women just be friends?

He caught the questioning look on her face. Her lips opened, but he spoke before she could.

"I won't have time for lunch today."

"Did I ask about lunch?"

"No, but—"

"I happen to be too busy for lunch." Her sudden grin was like the sun bursting from behind a dark cloud on a snowy day. She tilted her head, and sing-songed her answer. "Had a request for a spring makeover at that big house just outside of town."

"Really?"

"The works." Her head nodded with each word, emphasizing the depth of her happiness. "They want to add spring colors to their interior, then we'll be moving outside to give the outside a renewal in color and design. I'm really pumped."

"I'd say. That is big news. Still have the Campbell brothers helping with the landscaping?"

"Oh, yeah. Ryle said he could help a few hours a day too."

"He's a good person, a little too quiet at times, but good."

"Too quiet. Never talks about his past. Never lets anyone get too close. I get the feeling there's something from his past he's hiding."

"Maybe it's a person."

"As in a girl? Maybe, but he does have a mystery about him that's attractive. Those dark, brooding types always do."

"Are you kidding me? That's crazy."

"Maybe. Maybe not. Anyhow, I do like him. I'm glad he moved here."

Had her eyes shifted away from him? Maybe his suspicion she was interested in taking their relationship further was wrong. Was Amy interested in Ryle?

That was an interesting—no, uncomfortable—thought.

"Me, too. He fits right into our community. Wish he'd take a part in our play."

"He'd be so-o-o great as the lead man." A long, drawn out sigh escaped her lips. "I'd so love to find out that mystery though."

Uh, oh. Too many lingering o's in a girl's sentence was dangerous.

"What? And cast me out? Do I sense that the fairest maiden in Appleton loathes my performance?"

Her eyes snapped their sudden merriment at him. "Of course not, Silly. You're the best, but it would be nice to know more about him."

"We might wish we didn't."

"True." She slipped her arm through his. "I almost forgot what I stopped by for. You think I could find ten, inexpensive, but delightful-looking vases, jars, whatever, to use?"

That was it then. She'd been around Caroline way too much and gotten stung by the mystery bug. Still, the relief flooding his insides didn't bode well for his heart. He'd better walk a bit easier around her.

He pulled his arm away—gently. "If you're going to have a go at that cabinet, I'll see what vases I have stored. Sure I'll have what you need."

He headed for the front room. He knew just where to look for what Amy wanted.

~*~

That man. Amy watched Toby walk—or was it running?—away from her. Again.

She'd loved him since the first year of high school when her parents had moved and made Appleton their town. He'd paid absolutely no attention to her, three years his junior. Hadn't even remembered her name until months after she'd returned from college with an associate degree in floral design and bachelor's in landscaping. If she'd thought those prestigious items would gain his attention, she'd been badly mistaken.

It'd only been when she'd joined the community theater that he'd noticed her, and that'd been Caroline's doing.

Even now, after months of "togetherness," she felt more like a best friend or a Gal-Friday, than a girlfriend.

Sighing, she turned her attention to the storage room and cabinet. Whatever the thief was after she'd love to find it. Maybe, then, Toby would appreciate her.

~*~

Toby collected the half dozen vases that he figured would be suitable for Amy's request, and settled them on the countertop. They weren't valuable but lovely and distinguished enough to fit right in at the big house outside of town.

The people's name was on the tip of his tongue, but he couldn't quite remember it. The place had sat empty for decades although someone had kept it presentable. Now, without any warning, the owners had promptly employed contractors to refinish and remodel it. Too bad they'd rejected Toni's construction bid. It'd been a hard blow on them the way carpenter work was down the last year, but Toni would survive as she always did.

"All done." Amy's words preceded her as she appeared in the doorway.

"Any luck?"

"Not unless you count dust mites and a very suspicious gob of some kind of objectionable something stuck to the bottom of one drawer. Ugh." Her petite nose wrinkled.

Toby cocked his head at her and tried to hide his teasing grin. "You got a sample, right? So we can check for—"

"You're crazy, you know that?" She bumped him with her shoulder and swung away. "Are these the vases you have?"

"Thought they might work."

"Hmmm." She picked up first one, then another, and finally set three of them aside and nodded at the others. "These will work great. I'm going to look around a bit. I remember seeing..." Her voice trailed off as she vanished around one of the aisles.

Toby grinned and sat down on the high chair behind the counter. He wanted to go over the last few receipts from the past auctions last month. He'd been too busy before... What if he'd accidentally bought something like a hidden Rembrandt? Ha, no such luck. Not that he particularly believed in such a thing. But who knew?

When the old-fashioned bell above the exterior door clanged the announcement of an entry, Toby looked up. Ryle Sadler strolled toward the counter.

"Hey, you're early."

"Yeah, finished that project I was telling you about last week. Thought you might need that auction stuff picked up a little early." Ryle ran a hand over his short-cut brown hair.

"Sure thing. If we can get all the stuff picked up today, then I can spend the rest of the week on itemizing it. Already have a buyer for those two eighteenth-century chairs."

Ryle headed to the garage, calling back. "I'll make sure the truck's ready to go then."

Toby stared after the young man. He'd sure been lucky the day Ryle Sadler had walked in wanting work. Quiet, a bit morose at times, he was still a hard worker and genuinely likeable.

"I'll take these two, too." Amy's voice preceded her as she hurried to the counter, her arms clutching the two huge vases.

"What on earth will you do with these old things?"

Amy's mouth opened but she didn't get the chance.

"Toby, you'd better come and look at this." Ryle appeared from the back of the store.

"What is it?" A stab of admonition hit Toby in his solar plexus.

With a jerk of his head, Ryle said nothing, and Toby followed him through the rear of the building to the connected garage area where Undiscovered Treasures' van and truck were kept when not in use.

"What—?"

The windows on the back doors were smashed. Not an accident. A definite break by someone with a purpose.

Chapter Five

Toby stood off to the side watching the group of investigative people wandering around the garage. Amy had insisted gently and with such concern in her beautiful eyes that calling Detective Eddie was the best thing for him to do, he'd given in. He'd put up with these break-ins long enough, she emphasized.

He wasn't quite sure she was right. What with Detective Eddie arriving with the newly acquired and bossy Appleton forensics specialist. She'd promptly given him a frown that had set him firmly back in first grade with the strict Miss Davis. Now, channeling his first grade behavior, he'd been afraid to venture far from the corner where he'd sought refuge from such an august figure. She looked nothing like the severe Miss Davis. Instead she was the picture of—in spite of her jumpsuit that covered her clothes—a fashion model.

Eddie and the fashion model were far more than he wanted at his business. Tim, the tow truck owner, moped at the entrance, waiting on a signal to haul off Toby's truck. The salesman who'd almost chewed off Toby's ear trying to make a window sale, sulked close beside Tim. Not that he'd called any of them.

He shifted his gaze to Amy, and he frowned even though his heart insisted on softening a bit. She was such a sweetheart...

Detective Eddie rose from where he squatted beside the specialist and ambled toward him.

He was a dopey-looking guy, but that look was deceiving. The guy was intelligent—a genuis in his work. He'd seen through several of Toby's mischievous teen deeds and kept his eye on him until Toby paid his dues to the town. Not many mischief makers got past the detective's attention.

"You been making some enemies, Tobe?"

"Who, me?"

"Your feet fit a limb?" Detective Eddie tossed back at him, smirking.

Toby gazed at his ten-and-a-half sized loafers. "Not yet. Who knows what might happen in the future?"

"Well, let me know when it does cause I want to take a picture for posterity."

The detective's dry comment had Toby grinning in spite of his annoyance from the van damage.

"Seriously, you got any idea who did this?"

"None."

"Did you tell him about the shop's break-ins?" Amy's voice preceded her.

He really did wish she'd not brought that up. "It's nothing."

Detective Eddie's sharp gaze questioned him, the short twig stuck in the corner of his lips wobbling. "Why don't you let me decide that?"

Uh, no. That was the last thing he wanted. Detective Eddie hanging around would be bad for business.

"Can't think of anything I need to report."

"And I can't help when I'm left out of the loop." Detective Eddie's dry comment left Toby tongue-tied for a response. Too much explanation and Eddie would be down his throat with questions. Too little, and he'd get that skeptical look again that said Toby was fooling no one.

Amy's mouth opened, but Toby beat her to it. "Amy, I thought you had to meet your clients an hour ago?"

For a second, Amy hesitated then nodded. "You're right. I'll give them a call on the way. If you need me, you know where to find me, Tobias Lee Gibson."

Uh, oh. Somewhere along the line she'd picked up his sister Caroline's habit of calling him by his full name when irritated.

As she headed to the front of the garage, she paused to speak to Ryle, who nodded, then without another look, left.

What had that been about?

~*~

"Hey, Toby, what on earth happened? I heard someone damaged your work van."

It was Toni-DeLuca Douglas.

Toby hit speaker phone and laid it on the countertop. "How did you hear about it so soon?"

"Is anything secret in this town?"

"Right. Someone smashed the back windows. Nothing was taken nor moved that I could tell, but I had the strongest feeling something was wrong."

"Besides the windows?"

"Yes, but I couldn't pinpoint the problem. Still nags at me."

"Maybe you'll remember in the middle of the night."

"Probably."

"Wanted to remind you. Caro and Andy are

due back next week. You didn't forget?"

"Already?"

Toni laughed but scolded. "If I didn't know you, I'd think you were serious. Thankfully, Amy filled us in on how much you miss Caro."

What? How would she know? As good a friend as she was, he hadn't shared that.

"So why'd you call?"

"Besides checking on the van damage and reminding you of your sister's return? Oh, almost forgot. Starli and I, and some of the others, are putting a *welcome home* party together for next Thursday at Apple Blossoms. They're getting home late Wednesday, and we figured they'd be tired after the flight. Reserve the date."

"Do they really need a *welcome home* party?"

"Silly. You know they do. Starli and I have missed them so much."

"Since you're twisting my arm, I'll be there, but don't expect me to buy them presents. I could do with a nice gift for me from France."

"T-o-by...I happen to know she loves that tote bag in Sharon's Favorites but won't pay the money for it. Perfect gift for her."

"How much?" Twisting his arm to attend this affair for his *sister* and now new brother-in-law was one thing. But buying her a gift...it wasn't her birthday. And he hated shopping at Appleton's only fine department store.

"Don't worry. I'm sure Caro won't forget to bring you some expensive cologne or a new jacket."

Trapped. Toni was a gentle soul, but she sure knew how to make a fellow feel ashamed.

"All right. I'll check it out."

"And don't forget to get something for Andy. You'll know more of what he'll want than me."

The tone in her voice warned him she was serious.

Worse and worse. But why was he grumping? He knew deep down he'd do something for them.

But missing them didn't mean he had to rob the bank for them. He chuckled.

He almost hit the off button, when she spoke again.

"I've got the tentative plans drawn up for that building beside yours. Got time to look at them today or tomorrow?"

"Sure, what about later today?"

"Sounds good. You have practice tonight?"

"Six sharp."

"Then why don't I stop by around four? That should give us time to go over them briefly."

"Works for me."

"Okay, see you then."

Toni disconnected, and Toby shoved his phone into his jean back pocket. He sighed. The rest of the week he was busy. An auction Friday night, practice two other nights, and he had to finish his taxes and decide what to do about the load of items he'd bought at the last auction.

Might as well get those presents bought this morning before lunch. Ryle was in the storeroom trying to get a head start on that piled up furniture.

Toby headed to the room and stood watching the new man in town. Ryle Sadler was thin, but strong, by the looks of the muscles straining his shirt sleeves. He wasn't much of a talker, at least, to him, but he was good with the young people at youth services—Caro and Andy had insisted—and invaluable here at the shop and at the play practices.

"Would you mind watching the shop for an hour or so? I've got to go out for a bit."

"Will do. Almost finished here, but doesn't look like I've made much progress. You're going to need the garage to store some of this stuff."

"Yeah. That's what I was afraid of. We'll take care of it later today."

He wasn't sure how much more he could pile on the load of things he was planning on taking care of *later today*.

He'd worry about that after awhile. Right now, he wanted to forget it all. Forget Amy had bid on his dream property—albeit its shabby shape. Forget that someone was searching for something in his business, and he had no idea what.

Maybe shopping—as much as he hated it—would take his mind off his problems for a fraction of time.

~*~

It didn't take that long to find the tote bag Toni had insisted Caroline wanted, but just as he reached for the bag, a hand clasped the opposite side of the handle. He glanced first at the hand, then up...to stare at Amy Sanderson's twin.

Trouble was, Amy didn't have a twin. So who was this woman standing, smiling into his eyes as if she knew him?

"Sorry. I believe I took hold of the bag first." Toby insisted—albeit gently. He wasn't about to let someone else grab the only one left.

The woman smiled and withdrew her hand,

but he continued to stare at her.

Whereas Amy was short and shy, with a shade darker hair and blue-green eyes, this person was tall, almost as tall as him, with hair a light blond. She was dressed all in red and white, with heels that looked sky-high. Her confidence oozed from her like a sugar maple in the spring shed its liquid gold syrup.

So why had he thought this woman and Amy looked anything alike? "Do I know you?"

"I don't believe we've ever met."

"Sorry for staring. You look like a friend of mine. That must be why you seem familiar." Toby settled the tote closer to himself and released his grip. "Are you new in town?"

"Visiting. Work."

"I see."

In spite of her gorgeous looks, alluring smile and air of confidence, she sure didn't talk much.

"Maybe I'll see you around sometime. You didn't say what your name is."

"I didn't, did I? I'm sure we'll meet again soon." She gave him another quick smile and moved away.

Toby watched for a second. No, he'd been mistaken. This woman was nothing like Amy. Grabbing the tote, he headed to the checkout counter. "Hey, Sylvia, would you wrap this for me? I'll pick it up in a bit. I've gotta run."

Sylvia nodded, and Toby almost ran to the doors. Outside, he glanced around.

Across the street, Amy Sanderson was getting into her tiny, blue car. But Toby frowned. There was no sign of the tall, beautiful...and mysterious woman he'd just met.

~*~

"Toby! I forgot my script at home. Do you have an extra?" Sara, one of the secondary characters who played a teenager, pled with her eyes for Toby's forgiveness.

"Toby, I refuse to wear this outfit. Makes me look fat." Mrs. Birdie Sylvester, the town gossip who held the questionable record of being a widow the longest, was also the best actress in Appleton and hardly ever complained.

"I told you Tuesday if you didn't find someone else to play the part of Maria I was quitting." The threat in Jason's voice was convincing. Would he do really do it?

Toby swiveled his gaze from one to the other of the two main actors in his sister's newest play and sighed as he prepared himself mentally to soothe their high spirits and defuse their general dislike of the other.

"Really? You want me to quit? You can't even remember your lines let alone perform your character believably." Krissy, the female co-lead, was not about to back down.

First things first. Toby dug in a nearby box for yet another script. The girl was forever losing or leaving it at home. "Here's an extra script, Sara."

"I'll hold on to this one, I promise, Toby. You're the best." Sara waved the pages at him and trotted off to join the others.

"Birdie, you are not fat. You were picked for this character because of your ability to bring her to life. She's a crucial character and only you can carry the character correctly. Quit worrying about your looks."

"Are you sure?" But the woman nodded,

albeit a little doubtfully, and dutifully followed Sara to the others already on stage.

"Jason. Krissy." Crossing his arms, Toby surveyed the final two. "When we picked you two, you agreed to work together. I—we can't help it that you broke off your relationship right before we began this play. You agreed to not let that interfere with your acting."

"But—"

"Aren't you good enough actors to convince the audience you love someone you dislike? Other actors have done so even though they loath their co-lead. Some even despise their directors, but their acting is so talented, the audience never guesses their real feelings."

"Well..." Reluctance still edged Jason's voice.

Krissy had no doubts. She tossed her head and agreed. "*I* can do it."

"Good for you, Krissy." Toby knew if he was going to solve this problem he was going to have to be firm. He liked both of them, but their constant fighting was disrupting the others and getting on his nerves. It had to stop. "I'll give you ten minutes to get over there in the corner and work something out. No excuses. Do it. Otherwise—"

Would they? Could they? Their breakup had been the talk of the town for two weeks. Trouble was, it might have blown away, but rumor had it there was a new girl in town with an eye on Jason. Obviously, Krissy had heard the rumor along with everyone else.

"They still fighting?" Amy spoke as she and Ryle joined him.

"Yeah, Krissy seems willing to try, but Jason? Doesn't look good. If they can't stop quibbling, they'll ruin the play. The daggers they shoot at each other during their lines gives anything but a romantic feel."

"They'll come around." Amy patted his arm. "What can I do?"

"You up to repairing that wall that magically developed a hole last week?"

"Sure. You want Ryle to help me, or you have something else for him to do?"

"Ryle, I want you with me. Can you be the prompter today while I sit in the audience and watch the practice from afar?"

"Yep. Let me grab that script." In seconds, Ryle took his seat and studied the script he held.

Toby headed to a seat in the worn but still comfortable audience section. Preserving this old theater had been a dream come true. With some oldie but goodie classical plays and a few of Caroline's newer ones, most of the plays had been sold out with each performance. And, as an added bonus, all the proceeds, above expenses, went to local non-profit charities. Yeah, the actors weren't big name people, but they studied hard and did their best. Good people. Innocent and clean fun.

At least for tonight's practice, Jason and Krissy weren't glaring at each other and biting their lines as if crunching on hard candies. Krissy was giving her performance all she had, but Jason, though improved, was still a little stiff and robotic. He supposed even a small improvement was better than how they were doing before. And, as usual, Birdie was giving a fantastic display of motherly character concern. Good.

He wasn't sure when he became aware of a

presence, but a quick glance showed no one unconnected to the play within his sight. It was only when he rose to praise the actors on a good practice that he caught the vague impression of someone slipping from a dark corner and out the exterior doors.

Frowning, he wondered if his joking about a ghost thief at Undiscovered Treasures had befuddled his mind. He shook his head and moved to the stage.

It was past time to call it a night and head home to get some rest.

~*~

He didn't need an alarm clock. Once again, he gave thanks for the timer that consistently wafted the aroma of fresh ground coffee throughout his apartment. The percolating coffee pot had always wakened him right on time. Today was no exception.

Toby stretched and climbed out of his bed. Since Caroline had married Andy Carrington, he'd redone the small apartment and expanded it a little. Masculine, but with a touch of class and rich with history. Exactly suitable to his needs and likes.

For the present. Just until he bought the next door building. A big if.

Hanging pictures more to his taste—ones he'd previously set aside for a hopeful future use—rather than the ones Caroline had haphazardly hung about, and getting rid of all the unnecessary kitchen items he didn't want, had transformed the apartment into one of usability. The extra living space he wanted if he gained the next door place would project more of his character and tastes.

He poured his mug full of the steaming liquid—black—and strolled over to the window.

The street below was deserted, but that wasn't a surprise. It was early. Too early. None of the shops would open till nine—ten at the latest, and the two other shop owners who lodged over their businesses wouldn't be about yet. That let him enjoy the solitude all by his lonesome.

He was about to head to his bedroom to dress in running clothes when a large—almost limousine-sized—silver and black car crawled by.

He squinted, trying to make out the license plate, but at this distance, it was impossible. And his camera gear was in the closet where he kept it when not in use at the pre-auction viewings.

The car slowed to a stop, and a face from the back seat peered at his business. The gaze lifted, stopped at the sight of him, then—as if the driver had slammed on the gas—the limousine sped off.

What was that about? A potential customer checking to see the times Undiscovered Treasures opened? Or something else? Was he paranoid? Worried that anything different than his normal life was strange and suspicious?

Ten minutes later, Toby trotted down the street, straight to the town park.

Early spring, the birds were singing their hearts out. The trail was damp from the rain yesterday, but the sun was rising and the sky was clear. Perfect day to pick up those pieces he'd bought last week. If Tim had the back windows of his van replaced—as he'd promised.

The park was still empty as he finished his five-mile run, but he picked up speed as he re-entered the main park area. When he caught a glimpse of the same silver and black vehicle he'd seen earlier, he slowed. Jogging closer, he peered into the driver's window.

Empty.

He chuckled and turned his back on both the car and his suspicions.

~*~

Two days later, Toby sat in Charleston's auction house, midway between the front and back. This was the top class place in the state, and probably, way out of his price range. But who knew? Three months ago, he'd bid on a few items of seemingly less value than most of the things. He'd been pleased to find when he'd done his evaluation on the pieces he'd purchased, a few—though lacking the distinction of true relics—very nice pieces that would adorn some home with style and beauty. He was still refurbishing a couple, readying them for the huge upcoming Spring Fest and Sales Appleton put on every year.

He'd eyed a couple of items earlier, thinking they might stay in his bidding price range. But when they went up on the block, he was surprised at the rapid fire bidding and interest. He could barely keep up and had no time to check out who his opponents were other than the one seated in front of him to the right. An older man sat stiff and straight. A man beside him was bidding and only occasionally leaned closer to the older one, asking a quick question. The bidding went far above what the item was worth, and Toby finally shook his head.

When the auction was over—with Toby not succeeding in buying anything—he headed outside. He was unlocking the van when the voices on the other side halted his movement.

"You'll never have a penny of it. I'll see to that."

There was a low murmuring, then the voice spoke again.

"Nonsense. Rumors and suppositions, that's all you have. Get away from me."

"You'll be sorry. I'll find—"

The voice dipped, and Toby couldn't make out the words.

A car backfired, then screeched down the street.

Hurrying to the back of his van, Toby was just in time to see a sharp-looking tan car—a BMW?—turn the corner in the distance. But no one else loitered near. Had the first man disappeared?

Chapter Six

The old-fashioned doorbell rang later in the week, but before Toby could move to the main room, Amy's soft voice reached him. "Toby, need some help? I'm taking a break from jobs that stress me out."

"I'm in the storeroom, Amy. Come on in. This new job getting you down?"

"You could say that." Her sigh was like a breath of spring air. Sweet and fresh.

"What did you say their names were?"

"I didn't, but they are the semifamous Cowells.

"Right. I thought I'd heard the name in the past, but couldn't remember it."

The Cowells were known for their political achievements throughout the state. The elder patriarch had served one term as governor way back when. Even the children had taken their turns as various congressman and senators. There'd been whispers of some kind of scandal in the family, but nothing had ever been confirmed. The story had died the death of small-town rumors.

"Why on earth did they move to a small place like Appleton?"

"Our charm? Beautiful country? Friendly people?" Amy grinned. "Seriously, maybe they needed a break from city life. Maybe they'll only use this as a part-time home."

"Maybe."

"Whatever the reason, they're paying me

well, even if the old man is a pain. He's changed his mind twice already—after I purchased what he specifically ordered. Fortunately, the supplier agreed to a return as long as I reordered an equivalent amount in six months' time. That shouldn't be a problem so I gave in. By the time that was all done this morning, I was in no mood to work at Bloomin' Life even if I have tons of work to do there. I think I'm going to have to train another person to help with the work load."

"The perils of owning your own business. Thank God for insurance."

"Yeah. Wanna grab some lunch at The Coffee House? I heard they have their tuna on special this week." Amy flipped her hair over one shoulder, unknowingly luring him to do as she wished.

The gesture drew his attention, but he jerked his attention away. He wouldn't be drawn into any flirting games she tried.

But why not go? Hadn't they been friends since...well, whenever. She was a good sort. He was probably reading more into her actions than she meant. At least he hoped so.

~*~

Why hadn't her mother named her Annie Oakley? Every time she was with Toby anymore, she felt like she was fighting a gun battle.

A battle of the hearts. But instead of a historical gun-toting female, she was a modern, business woman with a forlorn love for a man who seemed to be denser than a block wall. The errant thought forced itself to the forefront of her mind. She jerked away, ostensibly to study a picture nearby, but secretly to hide the heat in her cheeks.

"So what's it to be? Going to pass up a chance for a good deal on your favorite sandwich?" She glanced at him over her shoulder.

"Are you sure that's all you're concerned about, Amy Sanderson?" Toby's honey-nut brown eyes laughed at her. "Or could it be you're a-hankering for that cranberry apple salad that's also on sale?"

"You think you have me figured out, do you? I'll have you know I've been a-hankering..." She deepened her cowboy drawl—mocking him—then slapped at his hand that lay close to hers on the countertop. "...for that turkey delight sandwich that's also on sale."

He crossed his arms and eyed her. "But which will the fair maiden choose?"

"You'll never know unless you decide—"

"Okay. Okay." Straightening, he laughed. "I give in. Let me lock up, then we'll eat."

The man moved about the room, not only for the process of locking up, but to tidy up his beloved shop. He'd never admit to it, but he was a bit of a fastidious person. A far cry from his sister, although she wasn't a slouch. But, as if he wanted to prove to his invisible opponents he was neither lazy in his work nor his person.

Smiling, she watched him give one final glance around before closing and locking the door.

"Ready? Let's walk." Toby pulled her arm through his and headed toward the corner.

"You miss Caroline?"

"Yeah. In some ways. But Andy's my best

friend, and they're happy. That's what matters." He glanced at her as if wondering why she'd ask.

She wasn't about to tell him she knew he missed his sister, that he was worried about the break-ins, and that the actors for this late spring's performance were giving him fits.

She wouldn't tell him any of that until after she'd helped him figure it all out. By then—hopefully, he'd realize just how much he loved her.

They started across the street when from the corner of her eye she spotted a dark object—a car—turning the corner.

"Hey, almost forgot. I wanted to ask you a question. I met a woman this morning—"

"Look out." Amy shoved Toby back to miss the black and silver car that sped through a red light. "Wow. That was close. Wonder if the driver is asleep."

"That looked like the car I saw outside my business early this morning. Gave me the impression he was casing the place."

"Casing?"

"As in scoping to find out the easiest way to break in."

"Are you thinking he's your—whatever. What is he anyway? Never takes anything and doesn't leave a mess—well, other than the broken van window. If it was the same person." She was talking way too much and fast. Careful, or he'd suspect she was trying to avoid the one question she was hoping he wouldn't ask.

"Here we are. Are you going for the special?" Toby pulled open the door, motioning for her to go ahead.

"Not order my very favorite sandwich in the whole world? Ha."

"Just what I thought." Toby teased then turned. "Headed to the men's room. I'll be right back."

"I'll get our table." She was still talking as she whirled, checking to see if their favorite one was empty. Without warning, Amy's feet slipped on the tile flooring, and she floundered.

A strong, firm hand gripped her elbow, stopping her descent to the floor. Amy looked up into two brown eyes. They were serious, even though the lips below them were smiling. And though they were handsome enough eyes, they weren't Toby's lighter, warmer ones.

"Are you all right?" The cultured voice carried the right amount of distant concern and interest.

Amy straightened. "Yes, I'm fine. Thank you."

"My pleasure." The man tilted his head slightly. He gave a quick glance around. "Are you with someone? Would you like to join me at my table?"

"Oh, no. Thanks, but Toby should be right back." This guy was very handsome. Maybe...

"Toby?"

"My friend." He should have been back by now. Had something happened to him? "We were planning on having lunch together, but he seems to have disappeared."

"I see. Since he has disappeared, then perhaps..."

One more glance around assured her that Toby was not here. Unless he'd abandoned her. No. he wouldn't. For a brief moment, worry raged with indignation, then reason returned. Wherever he'd vanished to, he had to have had a good reason. Tease that he was, he didn't pull mean tricks.

"Fine." Amy nodded, but couldn't stop another quick look and wondered if she should be worried?

~*~

Toby realized Amy hadn't heard him when he heard her startled gasp and turned.

Amy was engaged with talking to a man. Looked way too smooth a character which meant he'd better keep an eye on her, just in case. They seemed to be friendly enough. Maybe too much so. Toby frowned. Should he interrupt them? He glanced at The Woman and decided. A moment of talking with this mysterious stranger wouldn't hurt.

"Hi, there."

She was studying a folder, but looked up when he spoke and casually closed it. Her lips tipped up in a pleasant smile. "Hi."

"Mind if I sit?"

She waved a hand.

"I suppose if we're going to keep running into each other, we ought to introduce ourselves."

"Why? Isn't it much more mysterious to be—friends—not knowing?"

Her eyes coaxed him to allow her this.

He dipped his head and sat forward. "As you wish. Just so you know, I will find out. This is my town."

"Is it now? You say that with quite a bit of confidence."

"Any reason I shouldn't?"

"Not at all. I like a man who knows what he

wants and goes after it."

"Is that how you see me?"

She laughed. "That, and a whole lot more."

~*~

The stranger pulled out a seat for Amy, then settled into his own seat. "I'm Gordon Rickward, by the way."

"Amy Sanderson."

"Are you out of school?"

"By several years. I also have two college degrees, so I'm quite a grown up. Or at least I tell myself that often."

He chuckled. "I see. I suppose you live here?"

"Of course. Where else would I live?"

"It's rather a, uh, dinky little town."

"I disagree heartily. It's a perfectly beautiful community with friendly people and lots of interesting activities. I keep as busy as I want, and sometimes, too much so."

"I see."

Time to find out a little more about this guy. He seemed nice enough, but who knew in these days?

"Are you visiting? Passing through?"

"I thought I'd be working mostly, but now..." He paused and stared at her. "Now, I think I have a more interesting target."

"Target?" Was he talking about her? She wasn't at all sure she wanted to be described as a target, if that was the case.

"Target. I have just realized in the last few moments that my target is being a positive influence."

"I see."

"Do you?"

He was flirting. If only Toby was here to see it.

~*~

Thirty minutes later, Toby caught a glimpse of Amy leaving the cafe. With a quick good-bye to The Woman, Toby hurried to follow his friend.

"Who was the new guy?"

"Where have you been? You vanish for an hour and then come running up to me with unimportant questions?"

"I—"

"I was rescued—when I almost fell on that slippery tile—by a handsome man. Quite gave my heart a start."

"You fell? That floor will be the death of someone someday."

"I didn't *fall*. Gordon caught me in the nick of time."

That definitely was some tense insistence. He gave her a quick glance. Her cheeks were flushed, but otherwise she looked like her usual self.

"If you didn't fall, then why did he need to catch you? Was he getting fresh—"

"Don't be silly. He was every bit the gentleman and handsome to boot."

Was she trying to make him jealous by throwing a javelin of personal opinion at him? Ha. That wouldn't work.

Then what was that prick of hurt deep inside him?

"I told you I was going to the men's room then saw someone I knew. Stepped over to the table to speak to her. Before I sat down to talk to her, I checked, and you had settled at our table with someone I didn't know. Gordon who?"

"That makes no difference right now. I didn't hear a word you said."

"Really?"

"Do you think I'm lying to you? Why would I do that? I can't believe this."

Neither could he. This conversation seemed headed for disaster.

He'd seen Amy leaving the restaurant and realized it was not only past time for him to get back to work, but he needed to make sure she was okay. His innocent question had led to this first major argument that he could ever remember between them.

The question was: why was she being so touchy? He had spoken to her. Or, at least he'd thought he'd done so. Was he remembering wrong? Had he been so focused on The Woman—whose name he still didn't know—that he'd taken off without verbally speaking to Amy?

Or had she heard and ignored him?

She had seemed to know the man and be having a good time. He'd thought—well, maybe it was hoped, if he'd thought at all—that she'd rather spend the time with someone she knew as to play second fiddle—no, he'd never consider her that.

Maybe, just maybe, he was in the wrong here. Time to make amends.

"Listen, Amy, I'm sorry. I should have made sure you heard me. But when I saw a person I'd just met, I wanted to speak to her—"

"Her?"

The icy tone in her voice didn't bode well for any hopes of reconciliation from her.

"I mean—"

"Exactly what do you mean, Toby? You couldn't be bothered to make sure I was all right, let alone leaving without including me in your sudden change of heart?"

"But I did..."

She flung him an irritated look and hailed the only taxi Appleton sported. "Good-bye."

Toby propped his hands on his hips and stared after her.

She didn't bother looking back at him.

~*~

Toby turned the corner and slowed his brisk walk.

Lunch had been interesting with The Woman. Who knew? She could be a crime boss's daughter or the FBI, and he'd been blabbing about everything and everyone he'd known from kindergarten. Stupid.

He really couldn't get over how much she looked like Amy, only more sophisticated. Not that Amy had to take a second seat to anyone. She was always a top notch dresser, but more casual.

The Woman was playing a game. He couldn't begin to guess why, but obviously it amused her. That was okay for now, but eventually, he'd find out the truth, with or without her help.

He really hoped she was on the level.

A black and silver car sat in front of his business. A few feet away stood an elderly man. Toby assumed the man leaning against the car, legs crossed, was the chauffeur.

The same car he'd seen earlier this week.

Maybe his store had caught their attention and they were anxious to scoop up some antiques?

Or not.

As he drew closer, he recognized the man, sort of, and raised his voice. "Are you waiting for me?"

The elderly man peered over his glasses. Was that a glare he was directing at Toby?

"Why else would I be standing out in this sun?"

"The store closes from one to two for lunch."

The man pulled out an expensive looking pocket watch, snapped open the cover and studied it before raising his gaze again. "Two minutes past."

Toby flipped a quick glance at his own watch. "Mine says I have one minute to reopen those doors."

"You'd take the word of a cheap time piece over one that is priceless in value?" The snarl was contentious, yet an underlying, unexplainable something lay hidden through the tone-threads of the question.

Refusing to argue with the man—after all, he could be a potential customer—he strode to the door, unlocked it, and held the door open. "Coming in?"

Even from the distance of ten feet, he could see the elderly man's lips move. Muttering? Whatever, he straightened and walked slowly up the sidewalk, never giving Toby a glance as he passed through the entry door.

"Are you looking for anything in particular?"

No answer.

"If you need anything, just ask."

Still no answer. And no indication the old man had even heard him. Should he yell? He'd certainly had no trouble hearing him outside so obviously he didn't want to talk. Fine. He had work to do. Better get on with it.

While Toby worked on the business files in the front room, he cast occasional glances at the man. A couple times he disappeared from view but Toby could hear him rustling and once, muttering.

The phone rang, and Toby caught up his cell.

"Toby. You haven't sold that big desk, have you?"

Amy? She was over her snit. The relief that flooded his heart was like the sweet, light scent of perfume Amy favored at times, only he knew it wasn't perfume filling his head. More like some kind of emotion. He must have been more upset at her irritation than he thought. At least she was talking to him again. But what had he thought? She'd never speak again? "No..."

"I want it. With some refurbishing, it will be perfect for old Cowell's office."

"Are you sure? It'll take some work, and a pretty song."

"Doesn't matter. He'll love it, whatever price."

"Then...sold."

He'd planned on doing the work on the desk himself. But this would save him that and the time. The people who'd bought it would surely hire a much faster company to refinish it. Nice little profit there.

He hopped off his stool and moved to the tiny fridge, pulled out a bottle of water, twisted off the cap. Downing a large portion of it, he pulled out a *sold* tag from a drawer and headed to the storage room to tag the desk. Then settling again at the front countertop, he opened his computer to finish the store's book work. Toni would arrive later today with those remodeling plans he was anxious to see.

Caught up in his work, Toby had almost—but not quite—forgotten about the man. When he walked up to the counter and tapped the cane he carried, Toby looked up.

"I'll give you five thousand for all the large pieces you have in your storage room."

Surely he'd heard wrong. Five thousand? He hadn't paid—well, maybe two—and that was stretching it a bit. Wait a minute. How many pieces was he talking about?

"What pieces are you talking about?"

The man's black-eyed glare would have shaken a less brave person. He swiped away the question with a flick of his hand. "Never mind. I want them all."

"Let's take a look." Toby didn't wait on him to follow, but he could hear the steps behind him.

Normally, Toby kept the storage room locked to keep out nosy customers. He didn't want potential nosy customers in here when the pieces hadn't been cataloged. Making a sale without knowing what an item was worth wasn't something he did.

And today was no different. He remembered distinctly locking the door before Amy and he had left for lunch.

He turned before entering the room.

"I always keep this door locked. How on earth did you get inside it?"

"It was open and unlocked."

"I know better. Besides, I assume you can read?" Toby pointed at the *Employees only* sign posted prominently on the door.

"Are you calling me a liar?" The old man huffed his anger, his eyes shooting darts of outrage at him.

Was he angry at Toby confronting him about the locked door or questioning his reading ability? Toby shrugged off the imaginary darts. "You cannot wander around wherever you want to go. This room is too crowded for old—customers to ramble in."

"Don't contradict me. I'll give you three thousand for the lot."

"You already offered five."

Surveying the area, Toby spotted at least six pieces that could be considered large, not counting the desk he'd just sold to Amy's clients. He walked among them, touched each one and gave a nod to the man watching from the doorway of the room. "Ten thousand for all of these."

"That's outrageous. I won't pay a penny more than seven." The man tapped his cane viciously on the floor.

"Nine."

"Eight."

"Sold. Six pieces, it is then."

"Seven. I want that old desk back in the corner too."

Before Toby could refuse, he spoke again. "I'll throw in another thousand."

Who was this man? What was it about these pieces of furniture that forced him to be so insistent about owning them?

"That desk has already been sold."

"I see." He stroked his chin as he studied

Toby. "I cannot coax you to renege on your agreement with this other person?"

"If I knew why it was so important to you...?"

"Nonsense." His snappy tone belied his casual action of swinging away from Toby, and he said nothing more.

Waiting on him to coax? The man would wait a long time.

"I'm having my home redone and don't want to put the cash into new pieces..."

Yeah. Yeah. As if he'd believe that. The man was so rich you could smell the scent of cold, hard cash on him.

"I'm sorry. I don't back out of deals I've made just because a more lucrative one comes along."

"Did you sign papers?"

That sly look in the faded eyes didn't bode well for the next few words that would come out of his mouth.

"No. But my word has always been good around here."

Anger flashed across the man's features. "You would snub my offer for *your word*? What did this invisible person offer? Fifty? A hundred dollars? Pshaw..."

"Sir, what's your name? I'm assuming you're not from around here. Otherwise, you'd know that my sister and I've built our business from scratch. We're known all over the state for good deals and honest sales. We've had quite a few tourists stop in, and they've been a first-hand advertisement for us because of the way we handle our shop."

"What's all this stupidity about?"

"Just that whether I made a good deal or not before you arrived this afternoon, I did make a deal to sell this desk..." Toby smoothed a hand over the old wooden piece of furniture. "...and sell it I will to that person. And for that matter, it's none of *your* business how *I* run my business. I'd love to sell you these other six pieces, if you want them. Otherwise, I have work to do."

For one long minute the man stared at him, but was that a twinkle in his eye?

"One thing I do like is a young man who knows his own mind, and you certainly seem to know yours. Much better than—never mind. No deal."

What? The old man was backing out of buying the six pieces because he wanted his own way?

"What's that?"

"I won't buy any of them. When I speak, I mean what I say. You need to learn that, young man, before the world runs right over you."

"If that means being dishonest with my loyal customers then I guess I'll have to suffer through it." Toby shrugged. He moved to leave but hesitated at the doorway, casting a glance back into the room.

The old man still stood inside, his back to Toby.

He'd miss that eight—nine—thousand. So be it. The money wasn't worth ruining his friendship with Amy.

He'd gone from boisterous spirits to a depressing low in an hour's time.

Too bad.

The man didn't follow Toby out of the storage room. But ten minutes later, he reappeared, and with a nonchalant gesture, the man tossed a check on Toby's countertop and left without speaking.

He still hadn't gotten a name so he looked down at the paper check he held.

In bold, dark letters the name stood out in the upper left corner.

Barnabas Cowell.

Chapter Seven

Barnabas Cowell had barely left when Toni Douglas walked in and with her was Starli Peterman-Blair. Both women were best friends with his sister.

"Who was that? I've never seen him around before." Toni laid down the thick folder she held and shook back her dark curly hair.

"I haven't either." Starli picked up a plain wooden sign with the words *Be happy* scrolled across it then laid it back on the shelf. "Do you know him, Toby?"

"Not really. He's Barnabas Cowell. He wanted a bunch of furniture from the storage room I haven't even inventoried yet."

"Really. I didn't think you usually allow customers in there." Toni slipped over to the small fridge, took out a bottle of water, and held it up to Starli, who shook her head.

"I don't. But Amy stopped by, and we left for lunch. I'm pretty sure I locked the door, but the old man says it was unlocked. He was quite a case. Refused to buy anything at first because I wouldn't sell a desk I'd already sold to someone else. Then minutes later, he tossed down a check without speaking. You know customers. Always on the lookout for a good buy. I think he couldn't resist."

The women laughed.

"Well, you do sell such things." Starli's usually serene voice held a hint of mischief in it.

"I guess I do. Come on. Let's settle at the table over there to look over those plans. I'm anxious to see them.

"Sure thing."

"I'm going to mosey around a bit. I'm aching to update my bath and looking for something unique to be the feature point." Starli headed to the back of the room.

Toby waved her away and settled down on a bar stool to study Toni's plans for the building next door—if he bought it.

~*~

He was early for rehearsal that evening, but it would give him time to look over the stage and see what additional pieces of furniture and accessories would be needed in the next few weeks. Ever since he'd begun directing the community plays, he'd donated items from Undiscovered Treasures. None were worth that much, but it gave him a lot of satisfaction knowing he'd been a vessel of use for good.

He missed Caroline. Her intuition in explaining the characters she created in the plays were priceless in helping the cast develop the best emotional responses. But she'd grandly—as was her usual reaction when she wanted to do more than what was in front of her—insisted he'd be fine without her help. He knew almost as much as she did.

Caroline didn't know her own value.

Still, it was kind of nice having the whole apartment to himself. And now, running the spring play without her input.

He made his way backstage to look for a lamp he'd thought they might be able to use. There were a lot of items tucked away but not the lamp he wanted. Maybe Amy or one of the others had moved it. No matter. He'd ask her later.

Minutes later, Toby heard the heavy double doors swish open, and he turned to see who was entering.

Amy, with two others trailing her, strode down one of the aisles. As she got closer, Toby could see the annoyed expression on her face.

"What's wrong?"

"Toby, meet my sister, Jazzi, and a friend of hers, Aaron."

"Why haven't I met this beauty before, Amy?" Toby extended a hand but wanted to gag. The strong, almost over-powering scent of a sweet, sweet perfume assaulted his nostrils.

"She's too busy to invite me to visit." Jazzi slipped a hand on her hip as she posed in a provocative move, her lips pouting in supposed sadness.

"You're the one who left. No one forced you to."

Amy's quiet, dry comment wasn't lost on Toby, but he decided to ignore it and studied the sister of his friend. He'd known Amy had a sister, but she'd spoken very little of her, and he'd never been curious enough to ask questions.

Her parents were friendly enough, the few times he'd met them, and though Amy had her own apartment at their home, she was always looking for something with more privacy. Somehow, she'd never found what she was looking for.

"She's rather stand-offish, don't you think?" Jazzi eyed her sister. "But then, she always was a bit better than me."

"Why do you do that?"

"Do what? Tell the truth? You know Heather and James always favored you."

"They're your parents. Can't you at least show them some respect? Just because you wanted to rebel at everything they wanted from you doesn't mean they don't love you."

Whoa. Amy's normally sweet and relaxed face was flushed, her eyes troubled—and was that shame peeking from behind her pupils? Never in a million years would he have guessed such tension in her family.

Jazzi wasn't the cute sister sweetheart that Amy was, but she was a beauty, in a sulky, spoiled way. And they'd just met. Who knew what else might be revealed if she stuck around?

"You don't have to be nasty. You might have to get used to me being around. Who knows? I may decide I like it here after all."

Time to intervene. "Who's your friend, Jazzi?"

"This guy?" Jazzi clutched the man's arm and cooed her words. "This is Aaron, the all-around person when you need something done. I haven't seen anything the big guy here can't do."

What was there to say to that? And the guy refused to look at him.

"Interesting."

"I heard your actors weren't doing so well. If you need replacements—people who'll give it all they've got—let me know. I've done a bit of acting and am pretty good. You know where to find me." Jazzi smirked at Toby. Turning away, she tugged on Aaron's arm. "Let's go, Big Guy."

There was no denying one thing. Jazzi Sanderson was not at all like her sister. In looks or actions.

"Are they gone?"

Toby turned at Amy's whisper behind him. "Yes, and with promises to fill in the vacant spots once Jason and Krissy quit."

Amy shook her head and bit her lip.

"Don't let it bother you. I doubt she means half what she says."

The look Amy cast at him was filled with distress and something else.

"She means every word she says." Amy cocked her head. "Unless she's prevaricating or if she's trying to push across one of her deceitful schemes."

"That bad?"

"Worse." Amy glanced off to the side as if too ashamed to look at him.

"What say we put troublesome relatives behind us and concentrate on practice? For now, that'll be a much healthier task than the other." Toby injected as much enthusiasm as he could into his words.

She smiled, but the worry lurked behind her eyes.

~*~

Why had Jazzi shown up now, of all times? She'd tried so hard to keep her out of her life here in Appleton. It'd been scary enough to deal with her sister on her own big-city turf. And her parents were no help. They went their blissful way, traveling, working and enjoying their empty-nest life.

Not that she begrudged them any of that. They'd been fantastic, if strict, parents, insisting on rules that neither of them had broken deliberately—until they'd reached their teens. That's when all the trouble started. Right after they'd moved to Appleton. Jazzi, three years Amy's senior, had refused college, had refused the offer of the apartment on their parent's property, had insisted she was disowning them—even though Amy knew she still accepted the monthly checks her parents deposited in Jazzi's account.

Somehow Jazzi had found out she was adopted. Not that that action had made any difference with her parents. They'd treated both of them the same, and sometimes—though she never would have voiced it—felt they favored Jazzi more than herself. Of course, her parents had always insisted it was because Jazzi was so much more needy than her.

Well, now Amy lived in the apartment, and she wasn't about to move out even if Jazzi wanted it. Her sister would have to find her own place until Amy could decide where and what would be her next place to live.

Stepping up her pace, Amy caught up with Toby as he headed toward the audience seats. "Sorry about the unpleasantness back there."

"Hey, don't worry about it." He drew her hand onto his arm. "You're like a kid sister to me. Caroline and I seldom fought. It was mostly my teasing her about everything, but she toughened up quickly. I don't like to see you unhappy."

Kid sister? Was that what he still thought of her? After all their talks and...and—what? There had been dinners and outings, but he'd never called any of them a date. She'd just assumed...

Wrongly, obviously.

She wanted to punch him, but she wasn't the punching type. And telling him her true feelings was a mistake. A big mistake. She wasn't about to do that. So what was there to do?

She grinned. Same as always. Keep on keeping on.

One day soon, his eyes would open, and he'd see what a valuable asset she was.

Amy chuckled and ignored the questioning glance Toby Lee Gibson sent her.

~*~

"No. No. No. Let's see you put some temper in that sentence. Krissy, you can do this. I've seen you act before, you know." Toby strode toward the stage and stared up at the young girl.

"But Jason is such a—"

"Never mind that. You do what you're supposed to do, and I'll take care of Jason."

The girl looked far from convinced.

Toby walked up the steps toward Krissy. He lowered his voice. "Listen, you need to stop focusing on Jason and pay attention to your own role here. You do know you're one of the best actors we have in this play, don't you? Besides—and don't let this get out—we have two agents who've promised to stop by on opening night. Who knows? You might just grab their attention. But you've got to forget about your feelings over this break-up between you two. Can you do that?"

"Are you serious about the agents? They really are coming?"

At his nod, she squealed. "You bet I can do

this. Just watch me."

"Good girl. You go!"

Satisfied that his pep talk had restored her enthusiasm, he gave the order to begin at the beginning of the scene. Toby settled once again in his front row seat.

This time the scene went much smoother. True to her word, Krissy put herself into the play, bringing that much-needed touch of inspiration into it.

She was good, and if she paid attention to her work instead of others—like Jason, who wasn't even close to being in the same league as Krissy—she'd go much farther.

It was nice to recruit some of Appleton's less important or noticeable citizens as actors. Some, though reluctant at first, proved to be the best he'd found. It was a meaningful gift he could give to the community and its denizens. Probably his favorite one.

Halfway through the practice, he noticed Ryle wasn't at his spot as prompter. He'd been there minutes ago. Was something wrong?

Slipping out of the theater seats, he headed to the back of the stage, behind the curtains and stage setting. Studying the area, he spotted Ryle just entering a small, corner room filled with furniture and miscellaneous other items to create the setting needed in the plays.

Toby felt the muscles in his face tighten. What on earth? He headed straight for the room.

"Ryle, what's going on? I need you to get back to prompting."

No reply, and no Ryle.

Staring around the room that he knew as

well as he did his own storage room at Undiscovered Treasures, he realized there was only two places to hide. But why would Ryle hide?

He edged toward the first one and got within a couple feet when the screen toppled toward him. Toby held up a hand to stop it from clobbering him on the side of the head, when a figure rushed past him, giving him a shove.

Shoving the screen out of the way, he ran after Ryle. Something was wrong.

By the time he got out of the room, the far back door was closing. Still, he might just catch—

"Toby? Is something wrong?"

Ryle. Toby whirled. "Where have you been?"

The young man's usually serene face was puckered into a frown. "What do you mean?"

"You weren't in the prompter's chair."

"I was sitting on the other side. I figured Jason needed more prompting than Krissy. She's doing a great job this evening."

"I see. Then we've got a break and entering, I think."

"Someone stole something?"

"No, but they sure were looking for it. Caught them back in the furniture room. Gave me a shove when I spoke and hightailed it out the back door. Don't think they found what they were looking for."

"Or didn't have time to grab it. But really, is there anything of value in there?"

"No. That's what's got me puzzled."

"I'll make sure everything is locked up tight tonight when I leave." Ryle shook his head. "I'd better get back to prompting."

"Yeah."

He liked Ryle, what he knew of him. When the man spoke, he said what he meant, and he was a hard worker.

Toby had never quizzed him on his background. Had trusted him instinctively and taken him on his word. Yet he had a feeling there was more to his background than Ryle gave away.

Why had Toby been so quick to think it was Ryle who was entering the storage room?

~*~

It was late, and Toby was ready for a relaxing hour here at home before turning in.

If only he didn't feel so antsy.

It wasn't the constant feuding between Jason and Krissy. He should be used to it by now, but he wasn't. After all his talks with them, his vague but real threats of dismissing them from the play, the past few years he'd taught them in church meant nothing, it seemed, to these two.

Unless Krissy heeded the encouragement he'd given her tonight. Looked like she might.

But that wasn't what was bothering him now.

And neither did Amy, her family and their squabbles. As much as it distressed him to see her hurting, it wasn't her family troubles nibbling at him.

The trespassing tonight was troublesome, but it wasn't even that nibbling at his senses.

What was it? He frowned, standing still, one hand resting on the store's countertop and studied his shop.

Nothing seemed out of place or missing, but something was wrong.

Fifteen minutes or so passed before he gave it up, double-checked all the locks and headed upstairs to his apartment. Not that the unease left him.

After downing a glass of water, he headed to his bedroom. It was time for bed and with the early start he wanted tomorrow, he hoped sleep wouldn't avoid him.

Stretching out on the bed, he groaned at the lumpiness of the mattress.

He'd felt so sorry for Amy tonight. Not because he thought she couldn't handle it, but the distress on her face bothered him and gave him the unusual desire to protect her.

She was a jewel and would make some guy a happy one. Someday.

Too bad her sister was such a jerk.

It was only when drowsiness crept close that Toby realized what had bothered him earlier.

Perfume. Heavy, sickening sweet perfume.

Jazzi Sanderson had reeked of the perfume, and that was the smell he'd detected downstairs. But that was nonsense. She'd never been in his store, and he'd certainly never met her before tonight.

Had his unconscious mind just remembered her perfume scent or had she really been in his store tonight while he was gone.

Crazy deduction. He'd locked the doors when he left earlier.

Hadn't he?

His brain was too befuddled right now to think.

Mumbling, he turned onto his side and allowed sleep to overtake him. He was much too tired to figure it out tonight.

Chapter Eight

"**W**here's my favorite brother?"

Toby looked up as the voice, and not so much the words, resonated through him. He forgot about the box of pictures he was sorting.

Caro was home.

Toby had no time to revel in it. The vision in front of him both disturbed and delighted him. His sister had turned into a glamorous lady. Not that she was plain at any time. But she preferred to keep herself low-key and down to earth.

Catching a movement from several feet behind her, Toby swiveled his gaze toward it.

His best friend, Andy Carrington, stood leaning against a display cabinet, grinning like he owned the world. No doubt he did with an art career that was bursting with success *and* married to Caro.

Caro, as everyone but Andy called her, ran toward Toby and threw her arms around him.

His arms clenched around her.

"Ouch. Too tight. Are you trying to smother me?" She drew back and smacked at his arm. But it was a loving swat, and Toby knew it. He hadn't lived with her all his life without realizing she was a tender-hearted person, albeit a little stubborn.

Toby chuckled. She *was* back. Same old Caro. Putting on a front when her emotions were too overwhelming.

"Just trying to show you I'm glad you're

back. Let me look at you again." He shook his head. "What did you do with my sister, you there?"

Andy grinned and stepped forward to get his own hug. When the two men were done back-slapping each other, Andy turned to stare at his wife. "I could hardly keep the men away from her—"

"I wouldn't know. Couldn't see anyone but my husband." Caro studied the shop as she spoke.

They were so in love, and Toby loved that. His best friend and only sister, married. But that didn't mean he had to let either of them know how it made him feel. No way. Caro, and maybe even Andy, would hold that over his head forever.

"Well, all I've got to say, you'd better keep a rain-check on her. She's a wild card."

"Toby. I haven't been back a day yet, and you're harassing me as if I'd never left. Maybe I should leave again and see how you like working another month without my help."

"Did just fine without—"

"Don't let him fool you, Caro."

It was Starli Peterman-Blair with Toni right behind her, both smiling like two Cheshire Cats.

Toby sputtered in protest.

"He's been moaning and groaning ever since you left that he's tired of doing all the work." Toni chimed in and laughed out loud when Toby scowled at her.

"They're making up tales, Caro. I did just fine by myself."

"Oh, so you didn't need me? I could—"

"I have something for you."

"You do?" Caro squealed.

"Toby, not now. I thought you were saving them for—well, you know what." Toni frowned at him.

"For what?"

As usual, Caro's curiosity exceeded his own by far. She'd never let it go now.

"Caro, did you know you guys have your own ghost?" Starli interrupted their bickering.

"What? Did you see him, Toby?"

"Yep." He deepened his voice a bit to add to the intensity of his statement. "But how did you know, Starli?"

"How do you think? Toni filled me in."

"You guys are kidding. There are no such things as *ghosts*." Caro's eyes glowed, the excitement shining like a star.

"Are you sure?" Toby grinned and waggled his brows. "You agree, don't you, Andy?"

"Well...who says there are no ghosts?" Andy chuckled.

"Don't you dare side with him, Andy." Caro flashed a look at her husband.

"But the Bible does talk about spirits." Toby insisted.

"Not human ghosts definitely." Caro was just as insistent. "Beings that are fallen angels or angels from heaven."

"I agree with Caro." Starli added. "And I also believe God sends his angels for our protection."

"Well, none of *you* saw what I saw." It was so much fun to tease his sister even if he didn't believe it a ghost. He supposed he'd never grow out of teasing her.

"I can't believe a word he says. Starli, what

happened?" Caro cast her brother a disgusted look.

"He's had—what is it? Three? Four?—times when someone broke in the shop, but we don't know who it is. It's a joke, but he insists on calling the person a ghost. Poor Amy just rolls her eyes."

"Amy. Where is she?"

Toby shrugged. "Working, I suppose. I don't keep track of her every minute."

Caro gave him a long look. "I like her. A lot. She's patient and caring, and puts up with you. That's saying a lot."

"You'd better grab her, Toby. You'll find no one else to endure your jokes and all the gags you pull." Andy slammed a hand onto Toby's shoulder.

"I am not looking for anyone to endure my jokes. Amy's a nice girl, but not for me. I'm fine on my own and have no intention of settling down with anyone for a long time."

He spoke the words loudly, emphatically drowning out his friends' laughter and teasing. Somewhere during his denunciation of marriage, they'd shifted their positions, and the door to the shop stood in plain sight. That wouldn't have been so bad, but it was the figure just inside it that sent a dart of distress straight through his heart.

Loud at times, teasing and inclined to "like 'em and leave 'em" he'd never purposely hurt any of the women he'd dated. But the look on Amy's face told him this was one time he'd succeeded in doing so. He'd hurt her by denouncing any serious interest in her and by placing her firmly in a place a mite outside his and his friends circle of tight relationships.

He knew, and worse, she did too.

Amy was a sweet person and patient. She seldom spoke ill of anyone, but she wasn't a wuss. She could hold her own in any debate or argument, listening to the other person's words and understanding what they were saying, by replying in a manner to make them think in a different way. She was also fun to be around, and sang in the choir at church with occasional specials and filled in as the pianist when the regular couldn't make it.

He knew all this. So why had he had to go and hurt her feelings in front of everyone else?

~*~

Toby couldn't sleep. In fact, he'd never even lain down. Restless and upset, he wandered around the apartment that night, and finally grabbed a light jacket and headed outside. Maybe a walk would clear his mind.

Or not.

Why had he been so emphatic about Amy today? It'd served no purpose, hadn't fooled even one of his friends, and certainly not himself. He did care for Amy, just not in the way he suspected she wanted. All his obnoxious declaration had done was wound a tender soul, and that wasn't what he was about.

How many times had he drilled it into the teen boys at their church youth meetings to treat women with respect and manners? They were strong, yes, but that didn't excuse godly boys and men from behaving like ill-bred humans.

And he hadn't followed his own advice.

Unacceptable.

It was dark out, with no moon or stars tonight. Another spring rain was in the forecast, and probably before morning. Thankfully it was cool but not cold.

His feet took him—not in the direction of the park where he usually fled when pondering serious topics—but two buildings down where Amy's Bloomin' Life business stood. Besides the outdoor security lights, only two dim spotlights lit up the big front windows, emphasizing the gorgeousness of the arrangement showing.

He enjoyed them even though he had no idea how to create such beauty in his own business. Fortunately, Caro did, and what she didn't know how to do, she had Amy and two best friends to guide her in creating an enticing sales room to lure prospective customers.

Toby strolled around the building, not particularly studying it since the darkness prevented any minute scrutiny, but pondering over the owner. Why had she been so interested in buying the building between them?

Why not? His internal mediator was quick to ask the question. *Why should her reason be any less important than yours?*

But she didn't need it. Her business was booming, but she also had the space to hold the greenhouse, her equipment and plenty of room for her flower arrangements too.

What do you know? Your reasoning could be flawed. Is she not allowed to expand as you want to do?

Groaning wouldn't help anything, but his own personal mediator wasn't helping him calm down.

Besides, it's none of your business why. After the way you spoke about her today...

Gritting his teeth, Toby turned his back to Bloomin' Life and headed to his apartment and business. Enough was enough.

Tomorrow he'd have to find some way to atone for his careless comment.

Flowers? Candy?

No, too romantic.

A note?

Ugh. Too boring.

Or not. If he used the right words...

No, that wouldn't work. He'd be sure to not say enough or too much. Either way would be disastrous.

Why was he so upset over this? Maybe she was still laughing at his stupidity. Maybe she'd taken it with a grain of salt. Maybe she knew he was just flapping his jaws as usual.

This was ridiculous.

But as he entered his home, his persistent mind-mediator had the last say.

Maybe you hurt her too much this time, and she'll never talk to you again. What do you think of that?

His heart pinged with an emotional start.

That bothered him the most.

~*~

The predicted rain from the night before never materialized. Once again the weatherman had gotten it wrong or maybe God had shaken things up a bit to make life more interesting.

Either way, Toby was glad for the sunshine. Not only was it good for his mood, but it would be nice to work on spring cleaning the grounds today. Should be an easy day, so he might as well get it done. Caro had insisted on stopping by for at least part of the day. She could handle the inside while he and Ryle worked outside.

Once Caro showed up, he and Ryle gathered the tools they needed and moved outside. Toby explained what he wanted done: rake up the debris from winter, put new mulch in the flower beds and trim a couple of bushes.

"How's Amy doing?"

They'd worked for at least a half hour with neither of them talking, and that was fine with Toby. So when Ryle's voice interrupted his thoughts, he stopped raking and looked over at the young man who seldom initiated any conversation.

Ryle hadn't been there yesterday when he'd pulled the biggest blooper of his life time from somewhere in the depths of his stupidest self, so he couldn't be asking about that. Could he? Maybe word had gotten around. Great.

"Haven't spoken with her today. Suppose she's busy as always."

Good. Noncommittal and uninformative.

"Just asking. Saw her earlier with some guy I've never seen before. Thought perhaps it was a special speaker at church."

Irritation like thunder rolled through Toby. Why would Ryle think that?

But then that was better than an alternate reason, wasn't it? Toby gave the flower bed an especially vicious rake.

Grimacing, he shook his head.

"She seemed to be really happy. Laughing, and they must have stopped at Rita's cafe because they both held cups of coffee."

The thunder in his inner self turned to lightning. Toby dropped the rake and straightened, ready to tell Ryle it was none of his business nor Toby's. But the sight of a couple strolling down the sidewalk froze the words.

Amy and the man she'd been with at the diner last week when Toby had met the gorgeous blond, laughed their way past them. Him. Neither looked in his direction. Amy, closest to him, didn't bother to turn her head to even give him a nod. Or a wave. Or speak one word.

Great.

She *was* upset.

~*~

Amy had barely unlocked Bloomin' Life's door earlier when she heard the heavy door swish open again. She turned to look and recognized the man she'd met last week: Gordon—what was his last name?

Rickward, that was it.

She studied him as he walked toward her. He was handsome. And slender, almost with an effeminate look, but it could be his foreign-seeming speech that gave her the impression.

He must have thought she was displeased at seeing him, for his brow wrinkled slightly. "Am I disturbing your work? I thought the shop was open since the door was unlocked."

"No, not at all. I was contemplating how to best move that enormous work bench."

Ordinarily Amy would have asked for Toby or Ryle's help, but today...after yesterday?

Not yet. Maybe—never again.

Rickward studied the huge piece, then tilted

his head in Amy's direction, yet never taking his eyes from the bench as he walked around it. "Please. Allow me?"

"It's way too heavy for one person to move without scratching the floor."

He did look at her then. "I've lifted much heavier."

She certainly hoped so. Otherwise that expensive wood flooring would have to be touched up too.

The man shed his coat and laid it neatly over the back of a high-backed chair. He rolled the sleeves of his white, spotless shirt to his elbows and crouched slightly in front of the bench, again studying it. "Where do you want it?"

"I need it back a couple feet out of the way. The guys are doing some repairs and the bench is in the way."

He nodded and said nothing more. Then as if he'd suddenly downed a triple dose of an energy drink, he stretched out his arms, gripped the monstrosity and lifted.

Knowing her eyes must be wide with amazement, she watched him squat and lift, the muscles inside those dazzling white sleeves, straining against the fabric.

He took four short steps, stopped as if catching his breath, then slowly...slowly settled the bench in the perfect spot.

Amy wanted to clap, but she didn't.

He straightened and walked over to the chair in charge of his jacket. He dusted his hands, rolled down his sleeves and slipped into the jacket, shaking it a little, she supposed, so the collar would lie as he wanted. Only then did he look at her, his eyes twinkling.

"Anything else?"

"Thank you. That's quite enough for one day, especially for an almost-stranger."

His eyebrow lifted. "I thought perhaps after our lunch the other day we'd gone past the stranger part."

"I meant—"

He waved a hand, grinning. "It's fine. I was teasing a bit."

Of course he was.

"Do you mind if I walk around a little? I'm interested in your work."

"Please do. Would you like a cup of coffee? Fresh and the best brand I can get."

"I'd like that. No cream. Thanks."

Busying herself with preparing his coffee and refilling hers, she nevertheless stole quick glances at the figure weaving in and out of the rows of wreaths, vase-filled flowers and coolers full of fresh long stemmed roses.

She'd lifted the cups, preparing to join him in his exploration when he came around a corner.

"Lovely place you have here."

"I like it. Would you want to sit over there?"

"I have a better idea. Think you could have one of those girls back there watch the shop while you and I take a short walk? Do you have mugs with lids? Let's take our coffee with us and sit in your park awhile."

She shouldn't. She had tons of work to do. But the temptation was too great. The need to shake off those awful words from Toby was too overwhelming. Like an annoying merry-go-round that never stopped spinning, his words had played and replayed over and over in her mind all night.

It wasn't like she didn't know what he was like. Strong and well-built, Toby was so much like Caro in spirit who always was in trouble with speaking at the wrong time or not expressing what she meant in the right way. But Toby usually was more guarded. So she knew that if she'd quit listening to her heart and reasoned it out, she'd come to the right conclusion. He'd spoken before thinking of how it sounded. Still, she wasn't quite ready to forgive him yet. Soon, but not too soon.

Besides, this man was handsome and nice. Perhaps a trifle too handsome. Maybe manners that bordered on overboard, but she liked him, and he suited her purpose today. So, yes, she'd take that walk and hopefully slowly stroll past Undiscovered Treasures. With any kind of luck, or Godspeed, Toby would be looking out the window as she did so.

~*~

It couldn't have been more perfect than if she'd planned every detail. She'd hoped for but hadn't seriously thought it would work out the way it did—with Toby working outside at the exact moment she and Gordon walked by.

Funny how the pleasure she'd thought she'd experience wasn't there. It was all she could do to keep her head turned, ignoring the man she'd loved since high school. She'd always thought—hoped—he'd someday feel the same. Maybe it was time to move on?

It was only after Gordon had gone, exacting a promise for a "real" dinner later in the week, that the girl who'd taken over for her approached her.

"What is it, Krissy?"

"I'm not sure it's important, but an older, handsome man came in and kept asking questions. Then he wandered around."

"That's not unusual."

"When I asked him if I could help, he said, 'No.' It's where he looked that was odd. Under benches. Behind empty vases. He even opened up the coolers and appeared to be searching through them."

"That is odd. Did he say anything else?"

"No. He didn't buy anything either." Krissy seemed upset that the man had taken her time without any sales out of it.

"You get all kinds. Don't worry about it. He probably wanted something we didn't have. Or less expensive."

The girl nodded and left to continue her work in the nursery.

But Amy stared down at her work table. What had the person wanted? She hadn't wanted to frighten Krissy, but she *was* alarmed. With Toby's break-ins, surely it wasn't the same person looking for who knew what. But maybe this was just a weird happenstance instance. Toby hadn't had a break-in in days. This couldn't be linked to his troubles.

It was time to shake off her jitters. She'd had a pleasant hour with Gordon, but she couldn't dwell on yesterday's hurt, today's strange man or the break-ins. She had work to do and had never been known to be a slacker.

She had a good four hours' work ahead of her to get the table decorations ready for the up-and-coming wedding dinner for a customer in Charleston. But she'd barely gotten started when the door swung open.

Toby Gibson stood there.

~*~

He couldn't let this go. He had to make things right between him and Amy. It was the only Christian thing to do, the biblical thing to do. What kind of example was he when his remark had hurt another person, another friend, a fellow church member?

Regardless of his feelings—or not—toward Amy, he would do the right thing. Now.

He gave it a half hour to make sure the guy was gone, then headed straight to Bloomin' Life. As he approached, he hesitated, unsure of what to say, *how* to make it right. He couldn't see her through the huge windows, but unless she'd had to go out, she was in there somewhere.

He gripped the handle and opened the door.

~*~

"Come in, Toby. But I can't talk. I have fifty table decorations to make for a wedding dinner. It's tomorrow, and I have my work cut out to get it done."

"Anything I can do to help?"

Amy couldn't look at him. The words from yesterday blared like a trumpet in her mind.

Amy's a nice girl, but not for me.

"No, I'm good. Krissy's here if I need extra hands."

"Amy, I—"

She looked at him then. Really looked. His face was miserable, but she couldn't let him finish. She had to sort out why he'd said what he did, if he was serious or just trying to stop the teasing. Did he really think she was just a 'good girl'?

"Toby, I can't do this right now. I'm sorry, but I'm too busy to focus on...on what you think you need to say."

"I wanted to—"

"Not now please."

Silence.

Amy wanted to look at him. Check to see his reaction. But she did neither. She wouldn't be able to bear the distressed expression sure to be across his features. But what if there wasn't? What if he was relieved? He'd tried to make amends, and if he thought he'd tried, been rejected, so be it?

Raising her gaze, she realized it was too late to call him back. The front door slammed shut, and all she could see was the back of him striding down the walk.

Chapter Nine

Toby stood staring out the window. It was almost time for him to leave if he was going to be on time for Caro and Andy's homecoming party. Starli had scheduled the evening at Apple Blossoms, her classy restaurant, in advance, for their friends, although he knew not many town folks, if any, weren't welcome.

He planned on walking, giving himself more time on how to react when he saw Amy. And she'd be there. Caro adored her, and the rest followed Caro's lead.

What if he was making more of this than it was? Saying someone was a "good girl" wasn't a bad thing.

Too bad he didn't believe it. It wasn't so much the words, but the way he'd said them. It'd been clear to him, and he was sure everyone else understood his meaning. She was not now nor ever would be special to him.

But she *was* a very special friend.

Friend. Not a potential marital prospect. Friend.

Making sure the doors were locked, Toby headed down the street. He hadn't gone twenty feet when Amy's hot pink Mustang backed out of Bloomin' Life's driveway. For a heart-stopping moment, he thought for sure she planned on waiting for him. But then a hand waved at him, and she sped off.

He should have driven.

Fifteen minutes later, he opened the door to Apple Blossoms. He wasn't late, but already a horde of people filled the big party room. Manny stood by the entrance and greeted him with his overly English accent and manners that would straighten a soldier's shoulders.

"And how are you this evening, Mr. Gibson?"

"Good. Is everyone here?"

The poker-straight manager gave out the smallest of chuckles. "Not by a long shot."

They stood silent a moment.

"Miss Amy's over by the windows looking a little under the weather, if I may say so." The man spoke in a subdued voice.

"Really?" Toby studied the woman from afar. She'd worn a light pink dress with a feathery thin shawl. Her heels were bright and sassy—a far cry from the look on her face.

Without another word, he wove his way through the attendees, spoke when spoken to, and at last walked slowly up to her. The ridiculous thought of wrapping his arms around her and giving her a long hug flashed through his brain, but he waved a caution flag at that idea. He didn't want to be slapped.

"I hope you don't feel as bad as I do for that careless remark."

"Why would you think I feel bad?" She didn't look at him, only continued to study the fading light outside the building. "Do you really think I'm so shallow I'd allow jesting comments to hurt me?"

"I hope you're not. Just because I wanted to put off the teasing remarks, I made light of our friendship."

When she didn't respond, he went on. "Your—our—friendship means a lot to me."

"Friendship? I see."

"Why didn't you tell me there was a party going on tonight? Like always, keeping secrets from your sister. I should be used to it."

When had Jazzi snuck up on them? Had she heard their—his—conversation?

"This is a private party." Amy turned and shrugged. "How did you get in?"

"I told ole stiffy-boots I was your sister. That opened the door for me."

"And what about him?" Amy's face couldn't have been any more unhappy.

Coming toward them was Jazzi's friend, the Aaron fellow. He had on worn jeans and sport shoes, but his shirt was well-made and his long hair combed. Obviously they'd made an attempt to fit in.

"Don't make any trouble, Jazzi, please. These are my friends. They're not used to the shenanigans you pull."

"Shenanigans? Me? What do you think I am? Since you're so busy, I'm going to go and make the acquaintance of that perfectly gorgeous dude with the tiny dark-haired woman."

"Don't—" Amy's flushed face gave evidence of her distress.

But Jazzi ignored her and walked off, her Aaron following like a kite tail.

"Don't worry. She'll find out soon enough that Perrin has eyes for no one but Toni." Toby wanted to wipe the distress from Amy's voice.

A groan answered his words. "You don't know her. Wherever she goes, there's trouble. I'm so embarrassed."

Toby pulled her to him. "Our friends love you, and I happen to know that Caro adores you. They'll understand."

"Maybe." For a second, she leaned into him then pulled away. "I promised Starli I'd help a little."

O-kay. So much for apologies.

He looked around for Andy and saw him on the opposite side of the room. He headed that direction, speaking to one after another of his friends along the way and paused a couple of times to answer inquires of certain items available at Undiscovered Treasures.

Andy wore a dark blue suit—with no tie— that looked as expensive as Toby figured it was. His sandy-blond hair was perfectly styled. An afterthought had Toby grinning. He probably had had it done in Paris.

And his sister. She was a knock-out in blue, her best color. Someone, probably Amy, had created an exquisite corsage of daisies that grounded her and kept her from being someone he didn't know.

Both of them—Caro and Andy—were a welcome sight.

"How's my two favorite love-birds doing tonight? Were you surprised?"

"Did you have a hand in this, Tobias Lee?" Caro's voice was stern but the undercurrents of teasing sliced through her tone.

"Not I. Wouldn't waste money on such things when I can just give you a bear hug and slap Andy a dozen times on the shoulder to show my happiness for your return." He proceeded to carry out the comment while Caro shrieked in protest.

"Really? You're ruining my corsage."

"What's a bouquet compared to my affection

for a bothersome sister?" Toby joked loftily.

She sent him a dirty look, but it was downplayed when her lips twitched in amusement.

"Will you never grow up? You're going to be old and cranky before you realize you need to settle down with a sweet, smart girl like Amy. Otherwise you'll spend your last days alone and depressed."

"Can't you paint a more depressing scene? That one's getting kind of old."

Caro stood on tippy toes to kiss Andy. "I'm bored with my brother. Going to go talk with Starli and Toni for a much more stimulating conversation."

"Wow. She knows how to drag a guy through the pit of discouragement, doesn't she?" Toby made sure to speak loud enough for her to hear as he watched her departing back disappear among the array of attendees.

"She's right, you know. I'm wondering if you're allowing something precious slip through your nerveless fingers because of your fear of being tied down." Andy eyed him. "Marriage is not that bad, really."

"You do seem to have blossomed."

"Well...I wouldn't describe it like that." Andy laughed. "You want to grab a bite?"

"Not sure I'm hungry. You go ahead."

"Hmm. Sure sign of—"

"Shut up before I clobber you like I used to when you teased Caro unmercifully."

"I'm pretty sure I was the one who came to Caroline's rescue."

Toby waved him away.

He'd never tell even his best friend. But pondering Caro and Andy's words made a lot of sense tonight.

~*~

The party was winding down with only a few of their friends still lingering. Toby stood near the exterior door, eyeing his friends, when Amy came in from another door and paused, looking around as if searching. When her gaze lit on him, she walked straight to him, and Toby watched her come, the strange feeling of enormous pleasure sweeping through him.

She was talking before she reached him, her face revealing her emotions. Confusion. Perplexed. Fear.

"Toby. I can't find my key."

"Key? Which one?"

"Business. I know I had it on my key chain because I locked the front door when I left."

"Let me look."

She held them out to him, and he sorted through them.

"The chain seems to be a little loose. Are you sure—"

"Positive. You know I'm always careful." She was close to tears.

"You have another?"

"Of course, but not with me."

"I can break in."

"I don't want you to break in. I want to walk in like always."

"That is a problem."

"What the problem is: there's been a man hanging around."

"Amy. Why haven't you told me this? With the break-ins at my business, you can't afford to take anything unusual for granted.

"I haven't. I didn't see him, but Krissy said

he came in while I was gone the other day and snooped around, so I'm on the watch. And I did see a man lingering across the street twice yesterday, morning and night."

"Good. You have pepper spray?"

"Silly. Of course. I'm not helpless. I can take care of myself."

"You can. Have you stowed them anywhere here—maybe laid them down?"

"No. Yes, while I was helping Starli, but it was only for a half hour or so."

"Long enough someone could have slipped a key off the chain." Toby hoped that wasn't what happened. To think of someone running around with the ability to get inside her shop anytime when it wasn't open—it was downright scary. "Show me where."

"In her office. I tossed them on the middle of her desk. And I shut the door after myself when I left."

"Need I ask if it was locked?"

"Afraid not. I didn't expect anyone to be in that part of the restaurant."

Toby didn't have the heart to scold her. Not after she'd come to him for help. "Okay. Let's check it out."

"But—"

"No buts. We're going over every step you took from the time you left home. Otherwise, I'm going to have to insist you spend the night with Caro or one of the other girls. Or I can always wake up the manager of the hardware store to buy you a new lock. Your choice."

"Let's go look." Amy headed off toward the private office area, and Toby followed.

Toby kept his gaze fastened on the short hallway that led to Starli's office, but saw nothing out of place. At the office door, Amy knocked lightly then shoved open the door and flipped on the light.

"What are we looking for?"

"Anything unusual that shouldn't be here. Maybe some tiny scrap of paper or things moved out of place. I don't know. I'm not a detective."

Amy laughed. "If you're anything like Caro, you have the gift."

"I don't. You take the area over by the windows."

She nodded and Toby turned away. He wanted to look over Starli's desk. He wasn't about to pry in her drawers, and didn't think he'd have to. If anyone had been in here who shouldn't have been, then he hoped to spot it. Starli was too fastidious to leave a mess.

After ten minutes, Toby was ready to call it quits. "I give up. I don't see a thing different than the last time I was in here."

"Me either." She moved to the door, then paused. "Toby, I can't see a thing wrong, nor find anything out of place, but something bothers me."

"It does?" He looked at her standing perfectly still, her brow scrunched in a concentrating frown. "Any ideas?"

She rubbed a finger across her forehead. "I don't know...I think..." She closed her eyes.

"Is it your senses telling you something's wrong? That's what Caro says to do when I know things aren't right, but have no clue why."

Amy's eyes were still closed. "It's not my vision. I saw nothing that even comes close to making me uncomfortable."

"Hearing? Was there a subtle noise bothering you?"

"I don't think so. And I touched nothing that felt strange."

"The only thing left is your smell—"

Her eyelids popped open. "That's it. I can smell a very faint odor."

"Jazzi."

"No. She didn't have this perfume-y smell tonight."

"Didn't notice. What does it smell like?"

"You." Amy's gaze touched his and moved away.

"But that's crazy. I haven't been in this room for weeks. And only a couple times in the dining area. Much too busy."

"I know."

"Then...?"

"I have no clue. But that's what tickled my sense of smell. You didn't notice anyone else tonight wearing that brand of cologne?"

"Hardly. I wouldn't. I'm so used to it, it's second nature to me."

"You should mingle among the guests and see if your trusty nose targets the person."

"I can do that. What will you do?"

"I'll do the same, but can't guarantee I'll sniff anyone out." Amy's smile coaxed one from him too. "You're crazy, you know."

"But you love me anyway." Toby could have bitten his tongue off. How could he say such a thing?

"You'll do in a pinch." She flipped away from him, but tossed her comment over her shoulder.

Toby followed her as she hurried down the

hall, but his mind couldn't help wonder if she was putting him in his place, avoiding his awkward comment, or hiding her emotion. Either way, he was walking on a tightrope with comments like that.

Fifteen minutes later they met back in the lobby. Amy shook her head as she approached him. "Nothing."

"Me either."

"What's next?"

"Let's backtrack.

"How?"

"We've already searched through the restaurant as much as we can. Now we need to retrace your steps from the time you left your apartment. You had your keys tucked away before you entered?"

"Yes."

"Then let's search the entrance path back to your car. Could be one fell off."

"I doubt it, but I suppose we have to start somewhere."

"Right. Let's go." Toby took her arm and led her outside. Digging into his pocket, he pulled out a small flashlight as they walked to where she was parked. When they found nothing, he propped his hands on his hips. "That's a dead end."

"What next?"

"We'll search your car, then head for your apartment. Once we clear those areas, we'll move on to Bloomin' Life."

"Wanna ride?"

He cocked his head at her, a brow raised. "If not, you'll beat me there by five minutes."

"Five." She scoffed. "More like fifteen."

His heart bounced at her teasing. "Yeah. Yeah."

After searching through the car and finding no key, Toby tucked her into the driver's seat and moved around to the passenger side.

And of a sudden, everything felt—well, awkward. For the first time since he'd met her. They'd always been so conversationally easy with each other. Now, with those belittling words he'd spoken between them...

Still, she hadn't gone to any other person for help. That had to count for something, surely.

"Did you get the table decorations for the wedding done in time? He was pushing it to bring up the short time she'd put him off when he wanted to apologize.

"Had to work on them past midnight, but Ryle and Krissy both stayed with me, helping as much as they could."

"You must be worn out."

"Not at all. I allowed myself a couple hours extra sleep this morning."

"Good. So tell me about this man."

"Here we are. Do you mind if we hunt for the key? I don't want to have to call a key service if I don't need to."

"Sure. Let's go."

Amy's parents' lived just outside of town. Their property was spacious but not so much so that it overshadowed any of their neighbors. There was a visitors' cabin close by, and above the garage was a nice apartment—the one Amy called home. She'd lived there since finishing college, but now, she seemed to be antsy to own her own home.

And Toby understood that. As much as he loved the apartment he and Caro had shared since going on their own, he was restless to have a more spacious home. He hadn't heard back from his real estate agent yet concerning the property next door to his business. Fingers crossed, and the Lord willing, it would happen. Soon.

There was nothing to be found except quite a few footprints in the flower beds bordering the house, but Amy assured him she'd hired a crew to wash the windows. No doubt they'd provided the prints. That made sense, and Toby threw up mental hands in defeat.

Next stop: Bloomin' Life. If they found nothing there, it was a lost cause. Amy would have to bite the capsule of defeat.

When Amy pulled into the parking area of her business, Toby suggested, "Why don't you check out the windows and see what you can see inside, while I look around the grounds? It shouldn't take us long to figure out if anything's disturbed or not."

"Will do."

She started off, but Toby called after her. "Check all the doors too and make sure none have been tampered with."

She waved a hand at him and moved off.

Toby circled the grounds slowly. In the dark he knew he stood a chance of missing something. He'd given up on finding the key and was as sure as anything, Amy had either lost it or—his favorite, but unlikeable, suspicion—someone had stolen it.

It was in the area between Bloomin' Life and the empty building that Toby paused, leaning against the corner of Amy's business, staring up at the clear sky. A feeling of unusual—for him—melancholy swept through him.

But it didn't last long. From the corner of his eyes, he caught the vague sense of someone moving stealthily, hugging the vacant building.

Toby was in deep shadow and not moving, whereas the other person, though shadowed, crept toward the front of the building. Too dark to see who, but enough to tell Toby the person did not want to be seen.

Too bad.

Waiting till the person was almost opposite him, Toby sprang at the last minute at him, clutching at his clothing and hoping to get a firmer grasp. It was not to be.

With a swipe at Toby's arm, the person jerked away and ran with a long-legged stride toward the street.

But not before, Toby had clutched at and held onto one piece of clothing.

Toby watched the other one go, wishing he'd done better. Was this their trespasser? The key thief?

Moving to the outdoor spot lights, Toby glanced down at the piece of clothing he held.

A ball cap. Blue with green lettering blazed across the front.

~*~

Twenty minutes later, they gave it up, and Amy dialed the local key-making service. She motioned to Toby, and they settled on one of the concrete garden benches at the side of her business.

"I love this time of the night. Quiet, except for a few late night creatures finally settling in for their rest."

"It's the best time of the day. I get up early

to run, but it's the time after sunset till midnight that is magical." Toby reached for her hand. "I wouldn't say something so sissified to anyone other than a best friend."

"I know."

Her answer was soft and reassuring, and he savored the moment. Maybe she had forgiven him.

"Tell me about the lurker."

"I can't describe him much. He's tall and thin, gives me the impression he's younger—not old. The two times I've seen him, he's had a blue ball cap on, like that one..." Amy pointed at the one Toby held "...pulled low over his eyes. He dresses nondescript in black, or maybe dark blue or brown. I only saw him those two times. If he's the same man who came in when Krissy watched the shop, that will make three times he's been around."

"But didn't you say Krissy described the man as older?"

"You're right, so it can't be the same man."

"Still, you're description is pretty good. Has he tried to contact you?"

"No. And he doesn't seem threatening. Just leans against the building next door, almost as if he's resting."

"Maybe he is."

"Maybe, but I don't think so. I thought I caught him the second time using binoculars, but wasn't sure. It was cloudy and threatening to rain that day. I shrugged it off as imagination, and by the time I left, he was gone."

"Makes you uneasy?"

"It does a little. I'm not really afraid. Ryle's

around a lot. You're close by, the Campbell men are around off and on, and I try to be vigilant."

"Good." Toby let go of her hand. "Here comes the Key Master."

"Right. Keeton said he'd be here in ten minutes and always keeps his word." Amy stood. "I'll be okay now. Once he unlocks the door, I'll just check to make sure all is okay, then head home."

"I'd rather wait and check with you."

She dimpled at him. "If you insist, but you really don't have to."

"I insist."

The man had the door open in a matter of seconds, and once he'd gone, with a promise he'd be back tomorrow to change locks, Amy and Toby slipped inside Bloomin' Life. They paused at the door and looked around.

"Nothing seems to be disturbed."

Amy said nothing, but her gaze flittered around the room. "No...but something's wrong. I can sense it."

"More of a feeling?"

"Let me walk around..."

"Go ahead. I'll follow."

Amy wandered around the front room, pausing now and then. She stopped at the cut flower cooler. "The vases of roses have been moved."

"Are you sure?"

"Does a mother know when her child is coming down with a cold?" Amy flashed him a look. "Of course, I'm sure."

She moved on.

"And this. I never leave my pens lying out—"

"You were busy today?"

"Yes, but no matter. The pens go in their drawer. I hate messy counter tops."

"You've been hanging around me too long."

His friend laughed. "I'm afraid that habit was created a long time ago."

"Looks like everything else is okay. Let me move on to your greenhouse while you check your supply room. Okay?"

"Sure."

As soon as he was sure Amy was all right in the supply room, Toby headed to the greenhouse. It was a nice, quiet place, the part of Amy's business closest to the empty building between them. It received the morning sun which kept the room at a moist warm temperature, perfect for growing the flowers Amy didn't order in.

Almost before he'd gone five feet, he realized there had been disturbance here. Unlike the casual—could be overlooked—changes in the main room—this one was noticeable right away. Rows of plants had been disturbed. Plants torn up, dirt scooped out of pots, pots overturned and bags of mulch slashed were very real evidence that someone had broken in.

No question now. Someone had stolen Amy's key. But who? The person outside? And when?

~*~

Toby had always put on a front of bravura, hiding behind his jokes and toughness. Few ever caught a glimpse of the gentler side of him. That was one reason Amy loved him.

She wanted to be hurt over his silly words, but she really wasn't. She knew him too well. Had known when she heard them what lay behind his denunciation of love.

He was scared. Scared of committing. Afraid of making a wrong choice. Afraid of love. And though her feelings were hurt, his careless declaration in front of their friends hadn't fazed her love. Eventually...

"Amy, you'd better come in here."

Toby's sober voice pulled her from her thoughts.

"What is it?"

"Just come."

Frowning, she followed him to the greenhouse and stopped at the sight.

"Oh, no. What on earth?"

"It's a mess."

"But why, Toby? Why would someone do this?"

"I don't know for sure."

That thoughtful expression in his eyes gave him away. Suspicions were bubbling in that keen mind of his.

"But you can guess, can't you?"

"I don't want to get your hopes up."

"Hopes?"

"I have a glimmer of suspicion why there have been some strange incidents lately."

"But not who?"

He smiled, and Amy almost forgot her grievances against him, forgot her business was a mess.

"Tell me."

"I think we need to keep it between us for now."

"Agreed. This is so exciting."

"Exciting? Your business is a mess."

"It can be cleaned."

"I hope you're not expecting me..."

He was teasing. Normal for him.

"Of course, you have to help me. I need to open at ten sharp in the morning. Who else do I have to help me this time of the night?" She could give as well as take.

"Then I'd better tell you my theory so we can get at it."

She settled on one of the wooden benches close to the door that divided the greenhouse from the main business. "Sit and begin, kind sir."

"As you wish." He settled on the bench beside her. "I've been struggling with what someone has been searching for at Undiscovered Treasures."

"If they were searching."

"Right. But if they aren't, then why are they entering my business in the middle of the night?"

"Not to hurt you, or they would have already done that."

"Exactly. That's why I haven't wanted to drag Detective Eddie into this."

Amy leaned forward. "Then what are you thinking?"

"That someone is looking for something special. Something that's hidden and not in plain sight."

"I can see that, but Bloomin' Life? Why would they think I have what they want?"

"Have no idea."

"But you'll find out, I'm sure."

"With them breaking in here? And you at risk of getting hurt?"

Amy's heart picked up the beat to a tom-tom rate.

He was afraid for her.

Chapter Ten

Tuesday morning, the bell over the Undiscovered Treasures door ding-donged.

Toby and Ryle were moving some furniture someone had bought last week, and preparing to load it into the van, when in walked Jazzi and her friend, Aaron.

"Hi, Toby. Can we look around?"

"Sure. Help yourself. If you need anything, give me a holler. Ryle and I need to finish loading these pieces."

"You sell them?"

"Yep."

"Well, don't let us keep you."

Again, as before, the young man with her said nothing. Only stared at him—when he thought Toby wasn't watching—with his dark, brooding eyes.

Toby bent and lifted his end of the table, and the two men carried the piece out to the van. Once loaded, Ryle spoke up.

"Not sure you ought to leave those two alone in the store."

"Really?"

"Just saying, I'd keep my eye on them, if I owned the place."

"I want to check out one more thing while I'm in the garage. I had someone stop me the other day and ask if I had a specific antique tool. I'm thinking I had one I put back, not sure I wanted to sell it. Will you go ahead in and keep your eye on things for me?"

"As you wish."

Twenty minutes later, Toby located the tool, wrapped in a cloth, and hurried back into the shop. Ryle was at the counter.

"I'm almost positive they took one if not more items." Ryle's gaze was fastened on the retreating couple, arms locked together.

"Did you see them steal?"

"No. That's the problem. There were some furtive movements and his jacket pocket sure looked bulged, but I can't say that it wasn't that way when they entered."

"Let's take a look at the trinket shelf."

Two aisles over, the two men stood staring at the shelf.

"Does look a little bare." Toby rubbed his chin.

"Should we call Detective Eddie?"

"How will we prove it? There's such a conglomeration here—as always—I couldn't pinpoint what's missing if I wanted to. I really wish Caro would do away with this junk."

"Do away with what?"

Caro.

Toby turned. "I thought you were taking another week off."

"I am. Toni and I are shopping, and I know you told me to take the rest of the month off except when you need me, but I wanted to stop by and make sure the place isn't a disaster after being gone for over a month." Caro eyed her brother. "We were too busy the other day for me to check it out."

"I think it looks better. Cleaned out—I mean, we straightened up some..."

"I hear you." The threatening tone was

belied by the twinkle in his sister's eyes. "What are you two talking about here? We are *not* getting rid of the trinket shelf. It's very popular with certain age groups, far more so than some of the other items you keep in stock."

"Such as?" He couldn't help baiting her, and he sure wasn't going to make it easy for her to win this age-old argument they kept up.

"Never mind. Answer my question, Tobias Lee."

"I'm the one who thought a couple of customers might have stolen a few items." Ryle spoke up. "Toby and I were just scanning the shelf to see if anything was missing but afraid we're coming up blank."

"Hmm." Caro studied the shelf. "Unless you sold them, there's that bag of semi-precious stones gone, an antique brooch with questionable value, and a couple of large military buttons from World War Two."

"You've got to be kidding me. You actually know this or are you making it up as you go?" Toby couldn't believe she actually knew what was missing from this junk collection.

"Positive. Unless you sold it, it's not here." She nodded her head. "That's why I'm the salesperson and you're the buyer. I know my stock."

"Our stock."

She obviously decided to ignore his remark. "Do you know these two customers?"

There was no getting out of it. "Amy's sister Jazzi and her friend were in here minutes ago. As Ryle said, they acted suspiciously, and the guy's pockets were a little more bulky than when they entered. Or so it seemed. We really have no proof."

"Proof of what?" Amy called out as she walked toward them.

Toby winced. He hated to tell Amy their suspicions, but if he ignored her question, she'd know he was hiding something. Fortunately, he didn't have to do the telling.

"Amy." Caro swooped in for a hug. "I didn't know your sister was here in Appleton."

"I wish she wasn't."

Toby blinked at the sudden moisture in his eyes. Wouldn't do for anyone—especially Caro—to see him teary-eyed over Amy's sadness. He couldn't even imagine a fracas with Caro. Even with all their teasing from childhood up, they'd been close. They'd had to be. They were all they had.

"She crashed your welcome home party. You didn't see her?" The embarrassment in his friend's voice was real and heartbreaking.

Confusion registered on Caro's face. "No. But I was so busy visiting with everyone, I must have missed her. I wish I had. She can be a lot of fun."

Amy's voice was quiet and low. "I don't much care for her type of fun."

Caro rested her hand on Amy's shoulder for a brief moment of comfort. "I thought I saw her when I drove up, but she was climbing in a red car, and I didn't really see her face. Just that crazy hair she sports." Caro laughed. "She's a good person, Amy. Quit worrying over her so much. She'll find her way eventually."

"I don't have much faith anymore." Her sigh was drawn out as if she was trying to get her emotions under control. "I'm assuming you were talking about Jazzi, Toby. What did she do that you need proof? I'm so sorry."

"It's not your fault. We're not even positive she and her guy—?

"Aaron."

"Aaron did take anything. It's not valuable, just the principle of the thing."

"But stealing from my friends? That's unacceptable."

"Come on with me. I'm going to meet Toni at Apple Blossoms for lunch. Just you, me, Toni and Starli." Caro slung her arm around Amy.

"Oh, I'd love to, but I have two orders that need to be filled by this evening." Amy shook her head.

"Go, Amy. If Toby's done with me, I'll fill in for you till you finish," Ryle offered.

"Don't tempt me, but I'd better not. Not sure how your arrangements would turn out."

"You've got me there." Ryle followed Amy out the door.

Toby and Caro stood watching their friends, Ryle as he slipped into his truck and Amy as she headed back to her business.

"My heart breaks for her. Her parents loved Jazzi as much as Amy. I sometimes felt they went overboard trying to convince Jazzi they loved her the same." Caro picked up one of the trinkets, studied it and laid it back onto the shelf.

"I know, but what's there to do but encourage the girl? No one can make another's choices for them."

"True, but I want to."

"You're a strong woman, though."

"I've had to be with a brother like you."

Toby growled. "Get thee out of here. Remember your starving brother as you enjoy your lunch."

"Ha. I happen to know Amy's kept you supplied with food while I've been gone. And Starli and Toni did their share of keeping their eyes on you." Caro strolled toward the door but tossed back a final retort. "I have no worries about you ever starving, brother."

After Caro left, Toby wandered around the store, staring out the window at the building next door, thinking about Amy and her family—which, truth be told, he didn't know that well. The few times he'd met her parents, they'd been friendly enough although quite absorbed with their own travels, projects and concerns. Amy had said once her parents had always been obsessed with their work, that they'd been fair with their girls but quite insistent on their career choices.

According to Caro, their disappointment with Jazzi was well known in certain circles, but he'd never caught a hint of their feelings about Amy's choice.

The doorbell rang, bringing in a slew of customers, including The Woman he'd met at the cafe earlier in the month. She didn't make eye contact initially, only paused to rotate her gaze around the immediate area, a smile touching her lips now and then. Pleased? Or amused?

They hadn't shared names, so he was in the dark as much as he assumed she was, so was it happenstance or intent that led her here today?

"Hello, there." Toby called out as he approached her. "This is a nice surprise."

"Looks like you're quite busy today."

Toby grimaced. "It's spring. This is one of our busiest seasons, although for some reason Tuesdays are usually are slow days. And just when it'd be nice to sit down with a new friend."

"That's sweet." She dimpled at him. "Since you have so many customers, let me ramble around on my own. Do you mind?"

"Of course not. We can chat later." He nodded at her and headed toward a customer who was motioning for help.

Twenty minutes later, the woman had vanished. Where could she have gone? The customers had cleared, so Toby walked down the main aisle, glancing around. When he reached the other end of the main room, he heard her voice and paused.

"I'm telling you, Sir, I see nothing suspicious—"

A pause. An interrupted one.

"But you have no idea where it could be. How can I find it when you have no clue?"

Another lengthier pause.

"I know he's after it. Yes, I've seen him around town a time or two, but I haven't attempted contact. I will if necessary. I'll keep in touch. Good-bye."

The sigh that came next was long and—unless his imagination was working overtime—incredibly sad.

Toby edged closer to a wrought iron table and two chairs that Caro had decorated with an antique tea set. Free samples of name-brand contemporary tea filled an expensive, lined basket and sat close by for customers use if they wished. When he heard the soft tapping of her shoes on the wooden floor, he whirled and began rearranging the shelf of books.

"You have an interesting and charming shop." The Woman offered as she came into sight. "No wonder your shop ranks high on the list of successful businesses of West Virginia."

"You've looked it up?"

"Yes."

"Why?"

"I was asked to."

"You were? By whom?"

She grinned. "That I can't tell you. But I'm always interested in different things. Successful things."

"You're a business woman."

"That I am."

"Why is someone interested in my business?"

"They're not, per se."

"Meaning?"

She hesitated, staring at him.

What was she thinking? Why was it so hard to be upfront on the reason someone wanted to check up on his business? Could it have anything to do with the break-ins? That was crazy. He could not see this woman breaking in anywhere. He could imagine she'd be upfront and confidently go after whatever she wanted.

"Do you have plans tonight? Let's go to a nice restaurant for dinner. My treat." The Woman tilted her head much as a spoiled dog would do waiting for his treat.

"I don't mind—"

"I know, but I want to. Don't be difficult. Allow me."

"If you insist." Toby shrugged. "Apple

Blossoms is an excellent restaurant."

"Then I'll see you at seven."

"Seven it is."

For the first time in his life, a woman was buying dinner. Women did it all the time nowadays so it was no big deal.

Except to him.

~*~

Amy swiveled from side to side, staring at her image in the floor-length mirror. She was so glad she'd bought this dress from the clearance rack late last summer. The sea blue was one of her favorite colors and—if she did say so, herself—brought out the blue in her eyes.

Why Gordon Rickward had called now was beyond her. She'd almost declined the invitation to dine at Apple Blossoms, but Tuesday evenings were always boring since Toby never held practices on Tuesdays. Everyone should have time to spend with family and friends on the weekend and Tuesday evenings, he insisted. And he never swayed from that. So Mondays, Thursdays, and Saturday mornings or afternoons were filled with play practices.

Considering her options, she opted to go out, even with this man she barely knew. After all, it was just dinner.

Amy heard the doorbell as she gathered her wrap and a tiny bag. She hurried to the door and swung it open.

"Beautiful."

"I hope you're talking about me rather than my parents' home." She locked the door, and only then smiled up at him.

"By all means, I am. So you live with your

parents?" He guided her to his luxury BMW and helped her in the passenger seat.

"In word."

"And that means...?"

"They travel, and I'm lucky if I see them six weeks out of a year."

"No siblings?"

"One, but not around here."

"I see. Shall we take a spin around your lake? Our table's reserved for seven."

"Yes, please. I love the lake in the spring, although it's beautiful year around." Amy stared out the side window of his car. "Tell me about you."

A quick glance was the only response she got. At least for the moment.

"Come on, play fair. I shared a little with you. Now it's your turn. How else will we get to know each other?"

Gordon's mouth opened, closed, then spread in a grin. "You have a persuasive way."

"So I've been told."

"There's not much to tell. I come from a rich family, but my parents are gone, and I've lived with my grandfather some but now am on my own. He's grown grumpier as the years go by. Right now we're on the outs because of something I did he didn't like."

"Really? Was it that serious?"

"Not at all. He's a collector and by that I mean, not only valuables but worthless pieces that have little value, takes up space and that he doesn't seem to care about."

"Oh, dear. Sounds like someone hard to get along with. But I'm sure you love him and he you."

"Perhaps. My patience is wearing a little thin."

"He is family, and from what you say, the only one left."

"Trouble is, I asked him if I could get rid of some unnecessary things and he said yes. After I sold them, he raised the roof, insisting I'd gotten rid of valuable items."

"But you didn't."

"No. Pieces he declared ugly—and they were. He never used them and kept them in vacant rooms at the estate here in Appleton." Gordon sighed.

"And you're here now because..."

"Heard from a friend this is a delightful but quaint town and thought I'd spend some time here, hoping with enough time passing, he might relent his stubbornness."

"Have you heard from him?"

"Not yet. Maybe never."

"Well, give him more time. Don't despair." Amy patted his arm as they turned into Apple Blossom's Parking area.

He parked and swung open his door. "I won't, now that I've got a new interest."

Me? Amy wondered how strong his interest was. Reasonably, his life lay in a different town, a different direction. Hers lay right here in Appleton. Gordon was a nice enough man, she reckoned. Perhaps they would end up friends. She hoped he wasn't considering anything more.

They entered the restaurant, and Manny, Apple Blossom's English maître d met them.

"Good evening, Miss Amy. How are you?"

"Hi, Manny." She hugged him. "Looks like you're busy tonight."

"We are. But I made sure to save you your favorite seat."

"Thank you, but you do that for all your favorite people."

"I do." He cocked an eye at her. "But then I'm allowed to."

Gordon took her arm, and they followed Manny to their table. Half way there, Amy caught sight of Toby seated at a window seat with a blond across from him. She couldn't see the woman's face, but Toby's gaze lifted and met hers as they passed.

He tilted his head slightly, and the smallest of smiles crossed his lips. But it was the look in his eyes that bothered her.

Had it been embarrassment?

~*~

"Is something wrong?"

It took a few seconds for Toby to clear his head. Seeing Amy here with that good-looking dude had thrown him for a loop. Of course, he had no right to be upset—or to be embarrassed at being seen with another woman. As much as he respected and liked Amy, they were not a couple.

So why had he suddenly felt like a school boy caught in a mischievous act? Crazy.

"Sorry. I think I got lost in my own thoughts."

One perfect brow lifted. "I must be losing my touch."

"You? Hardly. Don't mind me. I have a lot on my mind."

"Want to share?"

"Too boring. Don't you think it's time we share our names? I've never spent time with a woman before without knowing her name."

"You don't think that will spoil the mysteriousness of our—uhm, relationship?"

"I think we should be past that."

"Right you are. You go first."

"Why do I have the feeling you already know it?"

"What makes you think that?"

"You seem like a woman who finds what she wants to know."

"You think I'm wanting to know your name desperately enough to search for it?" Her smile was teasing."

"I think you might work a conversation around till the other person innocently shared what you were after."

"You think I'm a scheming woman."

It was Toby's turn to lift a brow. If she wanted to play games, he was up for it. He would bet his business he'd had far more practice than she had.

"I do like my way, and I'm always prepared." She lowered her gaze then lifted it again.

The calculation in her eyes told Toby all he needed to know about her. She wouldn't easily lose any battle she engaged in.

She was speaking again, and Toby focused on her.

"I don't like being taken advantage of and have learned knowing more than my opponent—not that you are one—gives me an edge in business. That's why I'm so successful."

"And what is that business?"

"Oh, no. Not yet. You wanted to share names and since you refuse to go first, I will. It's Sharlene. Sharlene Miller."

"It fits you. And mine is Toby Gibson, which I suspect you already know."

"I confess. I knew your name before I came to town."

Why on earth was she searching for information about him before ever entering Appleton? Strange, but he'd play along.

"Am I to think my reputation precedes me?"

She laughed. "In a manner of speaking. Look, our meal is here."

And so it was. He was glad, in a way. Attractive as she was, there was something about her that bothered him. Her manners were impeccable, she seemed well-educated and confident, but the stealthiness—or whatever it was—was disturbing. He didn't like being around someone with whom he had to constantly be on guard. Something lurked in the background with her.

An hour later, he saw her to her car, and she waved as she sped off.

He drove home and parked, but instead of going straight inside, he lingered at the door, staring at the starlit sky.

Where was Amy right now? Still out with that man? They'd been nowhere in sight when he and Sharlene had taken their leave. Was she in bed, dreaming...of what?

That man?

For some reason, his stomach churned as if upset. Had the broccoli he'd eaten upset him?

Or was there another reason for his disturbance tonight?

Chapter Eleven

Later in the week, Toby was at his computer when the doorbell rang out its usual clangy alert of someone entering the store. His sister strode down the aisle toward him.

"What's going on?"

Toby closed the computer. "Nothing much. Doing some research on a few things."

She didn't need to know what things.

"I'm back to work today. Going bonkers at home, even though I love taking care of Andy."

"And what is the poor guy eating? You can't cook a lick."

Caro's nose lifted. "Says you. We had a feast yesterday prepared all by myself."

"What was it? Peanut butter sandwiches? You are famous for those." Toby jeered his answer and watched as his sister's face reddened.

"Phooey on you. It was roast with potatoes, carrots and onions. Can't go wrong with that."

"Really? Was it any good?"

"Ask Andy."

"You could have invited me."

"Nope. Heard you had a date last night. Who was the new girl?"

"You don't know her."

"I might."

"Sharlene Miller."

"You're right. I don't. What about Amy?"

"What about her?" Toby had the sense to give the door a quick glance. He didn't want

Amy appearing out of the blue and hearing his remarks.

"Tobias Lee, you are the densest man I have ever met."

"That's like the kettle calling the skillet black."

Caro settled on the stool next to him. "Tell me more about this new girl. Is she moving here? Is this just a casual fling?"

"I know as little as you do. We met a couple times, then she showed up here and invited me to dinner. Which we did. Said our good-byes with no declarations of meeting again. The end."

"You're not even the tiniest bit interested?"

"Nope. Well, not much anyhow."

"If I was Amy, I'd run as fast as I could away from you."

Toby played the indignant card. "Why? What have I done?"

"Never mind. You're hopeless. The ghost been around lately?"

"Not since two weeks ago. Not sure if he gave up, or found somewhere else more interesting."

"Still no idea why?"

"None."

Caro stood. "I'm going to check out those new glass containers you purchased a couple months ago. I think it's time to bring them out of hiding."

As soon as she'd disappeared, he flipped open his desktop again, and studied the page again.

Sharlene Miller, Attorney at Law.

Attorney? Sharlene? Why was she here in

Appleton? Who was her client? And why was she so friendly to him?

He needed to talk with someone, and who better than Amy? Andy had been a best friend since kindergarden, but he was busier now than ever with his painting getting more and more acclaim. He couldn't bother him with petty business like break-ins, ghosts and new people in town.

Toby punched in Amy's number, and when her voice answered, his heart lifted. Yeah, she had that effect on him.

"Hey, there. I need to discuss some things with you. Do you have any free time today?"

"Umm. Let me check my schedule. I see I have to finish the order I'm processing now, and this afternoon I need to check out the big project outside of town the Campbell boys are finishing up today. So that means I have from eleven to around two free. Will that time work?"

"Perfect. Lunch at The Coffee House?"

"No. Let's have a picnic at the lake. If you'll pick up some drinks, I've got leftover ham and turkey."

"With lots of trimmings?"

"How else are you supposed to eat leftovers?"

"Great. I'll swing by."

"Do we have time to walk?"

"Sure. With one basket and a tote for the drinks, we can be there in fifteen minutes."

"Then I'll meet you there. I've got a couple of stops I need to make first."

When Toby hung up, he called The Coffee House and ordered iced coffee and tea to be delivered right before he'd need to leave to meet Amy. As he hung up once again, Caro walked up to the checkout counter, a frown on her face. "What's wrong?"

"I can't find that small chest I asked Ryle and you to put back."

"Don't remember it."

"It was the one you bought last fall, and I planned to use it this spring for a treasure hunt during the Appleton Business Fair. I figured it might draw a bigger crowd to have a treasure chest filled with semi-precious items. Should give a super boost to our business."

"That's a great idea. I remember you mentioned something about that, but cannot remember where you wanted it hid."

"In the garage, Silly. You and Ryle placed it far back in the corner and covered it with an old tarp."

"Well, I haven't touched it. Check the garage again. Forgot all about it." Toby stood as the door opened again to allow The Coffee House delivery person to enter, carrying the drinks Toby had ordered. "Here are our drinks. I've got to go. Meeting someone."

"Really. This Sharlene person? I thought you weren't interested."

"Jeepers. Can't a guy change his mind?" Toby tweaked her chin as he passed her. "You'll have to watch the store. Won't be back for a couple hours."

"Really? I'm telling Amy."

"Go ahead."

"Aha. It's Amy you're meeting. You wouldn't be so nonchalant if it wasn't."

"Says you. Bye."

"Be good to her."

"I never treat a woman badly." He let the door swoosh behind him to keep her from making any more comments. He loved his sister, but her spot-on discernment unsettled him.

Amy had spread a quilt on the ground under a maple tree. She leaned against the trunk, a book in her hands, reading. Dapples of sunshine dribbled through the tree branches, highlighting her dark blond hair.

She'd taken time to gather a few wild spring flowers and placed them haphazardly in a small pop bottle she must have rescued from the trash. She'd torn off the wrapper and the translucent green blended well with the sunny yellow, printed skirt she was wearing.

It was a quiet scene, and if he'd been Andy—the painter—he would have drawn out his pencils and ink to sketch the scene.

But enough ruminating. He had things to talk about, and Amy was the best at listening. Much better than Andy, and definitely Caro.

"This is nice."

Amy looked up. "We haven't had a picnic in a long time. Figured we had time to do it right, if we're going to do one."

"I like it, but then there's not much you do that you don't do well."

"Thanks, I think."

"It's a compliment. I brought coffee and tea."

"Perfect. Sit." She waved a hand at the other end of the quilt. "Shall I read a chapter like I used to?"

"Do you mind if we talk?"

Amy placed the marker in the book and closed it. "Sure. Go ahead."

"Ever since that first break-in at the store,

I've been troubled by some things."

"Really? You haven't said anything. I thought you were taking it as a joke."

"I guess I had to stew about it. It was kind of funny calling the intruder a ghost, but not so much now. Especially after your break in."

"What are you thinking?"

"Someone is after something. I'm more sure of it than before, especially after what Caro told me this morning."

Amy sat forward. "Don't keep me in suspense. Give."

"Last fall I was at an auction over near Huntington. There was a small-ish chest that I got for a reasonable price. It was in good shape, so I figured we could sell it quickly. But once I got it home, Caro pounced on it and began storing certain items in it. Around Christmas time, she had Ryle and me hide it in the garage covered with a tarp. That's the last I thought about it."

"And?"

"It's missing. Or at least she thinks it is. I told her to check the garage again—it might have gotten moved. If she doesn't find it, then for sure, the person who damaged my truck took it."

"But why? Is there something valuable in it?"

"Not according to Caro. She said she'd been putting semi-precious items in it to prepare for a treasure hunt during the summer fair. I admit, doesn't sound like much of a motive for theft."

"Maybe not. But what about all the novels that talk about a secret place in chests? I don't suppose you searched it?"

"Afraid not. Looked empty and I took that on face value. Now I'm wondering if I should have done so."

"How could you have known? Except for reporting it to Detective Eddie, there wasn't much else to do."

"I don't want you to take any chances, Amy. With nothing missing until now—if it is—the theft, broken window on the van and destruction at Bloomin' Life, we could be dealing with a dangerous person. At least, willing to do structural damage if not bodily. And I'm not willing to rule that out yet."

"I understand. But the damage done was while I was gone. If they'd wanted to hurt me, then they would have broken in while I was at the shop."

"True. But if they haven't found what they're looking for, they might return more desperate than before."

"It's hard for me to believe that."

"It sounds farfetched, but a possibility, don't you think?"

"It's something to think about, true." Amy dug into the basket she'd brought and laid out thick-sliced bread loaded with ham, turkey, cheese and the works. Veggie strips with dip added the crunch they both enjoyed and the iced tea quenched their thirst.

When they'd finished, Toby helped her load up the basket and tucked the remainder of the drinks in the tote he'd carried it in. They stashed their goodies behind a thick bush and headed around the lake for a quick walk. Amy linked her arm in Toby's.

"Tell me, what should we do?"

"I have a plan."

"I figured as much. I hope it doesn't involve jumping from rooftop to rooftop after the thief."

Toby laughed. "No, but I almost did, when I caught someone in the building I'm hoping to buy soon."

"You mean the one I'm buying?"

"Really, Amy? That's not funny. You know how much I've wanted that building, but Joe wouldn't sell. Until now. Why your sudden interest? I've never heard a word from you about it, except encouraging me to go for it."

"I have my reasons, which I'm not sharing with you right now."

Toby wanted to be upset with her, but those last two words held a meaning. Whatever it was, she would tell all, hopefully, soon. Still, it was frustrating that she seemed so interested in it. Whether she had the money was questionable, but her credit was good, and her parents, he figured, would help out if she needed it.

He decided not to argue with her.

"Back to our intruder. Why don't we spread the rumor that we've bought a very valuable item at an auction, but plan on moving it later at the right time?"

"You think it will work?"

"Who knows? But I hate being manipulated. If this person wants it so badly, why doesn't he buy it from us?"

"Poor with no money probably."

"Or just despicably lazy or criminal."

"So we whisper this around our friends, hoping they'll pass along the information?"

"Won't hurt to try."

"Sounds like you're beginning to take this seriously."

"I am. The destruction at your business and the possible theft of the chest from mine, has me worried. I don't want you to get hurt."

"And I feel the same about you. I mean it *was* kind of funny at the beginning but not now. Detective Eddie is a good cop. Let's bring him in."

Amy's pleading eyes did more to convince him than her words. "Fine. I'll talk with him this evening."

"Goo—"

They'd rounded a bend in the path. Up ahead, just off the path, stood two people close together, talking in low tones. Not close enough he could hear their words, but their tone was anything but business.

"Isn't that the man you had dinner with?"

"And isn't that the woman you sat with at Apple Blossoms the other night?"

"Yes."

"Yes."

Amy's reply at the same time sent a smile to his lips.

"Wonder what's going on?" Toby rubbed his chin.

"I have no idea, but they sure look cozy."

"By the looks of it, they didn't just meet."

"Umm. What are they doing?"

He couldn't help it and let a chuckle escape. "I think that's called kissing."

~*~

Toby was still laughing over Amy's face.

Those two they'd seen on the path at the lake were either fast workers or knew each other already. Why were they both here in

Appleton sneaking around—or so it looked—to meet? And why had Sharlene seemed to want to meet him, and the same with that Gordon Rickward with Amy?

What kind of name was Rickward, anyway?

But that was petty thinking, and it didn't matter. What did was the relationship between two people who seemed strangers before. But then, perhaps this wasn't their first time together. Just because he hadn't seen them together before wasn't a good reason to suspect anything.

Caro and Ryle looked up when Toby re-entered Undiscovered Treasures. The look in their eyes didn't bode for good.

"What's up?"

"We've got another theft," Caro soberly told him.

"What?"

"A pair of antique lamps."

"*Lamps*? Which ones?"

"You bought them at the auction when Amy went with us a few weeks ago. Remember she bought the heavy bed, dresser and wardrobe?" Ryle pointed out.

"Do I? My back aches just thinking about those massive things."

"Right. You insisted on having them when she outbid you on the bedroom suit," Ryle reminded him.

"I didn't see them. Don't you have a picture of them?" Caro swept back a straggling lock of hair.

"Sure. In the records book."

"Let me take a look at it." Caro stretched out a hand for Toby to hand it over, then flipped through the pages. She stopped and stared at one. "These are the ones? Do you know what they are and how much they're worth?"

"That's why I'm in charge of the buying, or have you forgotten?"

Caro was an excellent salesperson. She could talk a snowman into buying more snow. But she was too unpredictable in the buying realm. Either she bought too much, period, or went on a spree of present interest in vanities or trinkets or...whatever caught her interest. She was better off sticking with what she did well—sales.

Caro's voice lowered to a whisper. Obviously, she'd decided to ignore his last statement.

"Who could have taken them?"

"I don't—"

For a second, Ryle's gaze shifted away from his, and Toby's heart sank. Was the young man hiding something? Did he know something he wasn't sharing?

Toby's mind skipped back to the person fleeing by rooftop from the building next door. He'd thought then it looked vaguely like Ryle's thin form. Was the suspicion correct?

"—know." He finished his sentence when Caro flashed him a look.

"If you have nothing else for me to do today, I've got a few things I need to finish up. Okay if I go?" Ryle straightened.

"Just going to finish the books, then go over a few of the auctions in the nearby area to see what gems we can bid on. There's a few interesting ones in the next couple weeks. You free to go to help me load?"

"Sure. Don't forget about those two estate

sales I mentioned to you."

"I won't. Thanks for your help today."

Ryle nodded and waved a hand as he left.

"I'm sure glad Ryle decided to make Appleton his home town." Caro smiled, then beamed as Andy entered.

"Me too. Wonder how he gets along. The light work load he takes on can't possibly pay his bills."

"Why the sudden interest in Ryle? He's proven himself a worthy citizen of Appleton. No one visiting would ever realize he's only been here a couple years."

"Right. But—"

"Come to rescue my bride." Andy's quiet voice interrupted their musing. "I know how hard she works."

"Yeah, right." Toby slapped Andy's back. "What are you doing in town this time of the day?"

"Figured my adorable wife forgot we have plans this evening. Why don't you and Amy join us? I received extra tickets because of donating a piece of work of mine for an auction to raise money for kids in need in Huntington. Come on, go. We haven't had time to catch up for awhile."

"Not sure Amy could make it. She had to do the final inspection on that big decorating project outside of town. She may not be finished in time."

"Check with her. We don't have to leave till five thirty. Still plenty of time." Andy took Caro's arm and led her to the door. "Give me a call."

They hadn't been to a formal outing in quite

some time. He'd shut down the shop for fifteen minutes and run over to Bloomin' Life and see what she thought.

The moment he stepped inside Amy's shop, he heard the crying.

"Amy, are you okay?"

She poked her head around the doorway to her office. "I'll be out in a sec. Got a problem here."

"Can I help?"

"Do you have extra tissues?" She grinned.

"Sorry. All out."

"Then I'll be out in a few."

It was a full twenty minutes later that Amy reappeared, shaking her head.

"What's going on? When I entered I thought it was you."

"No. It's Jazzi. Seems she and Aaron had a violent disagreement. She's threatening to disappear."

"As in leave him or as in vanish with no trace? That last is harder to do than a person realizes until you attempt it."

"You would know."

"Why does she want to run away?"

"That's Jazzi. She ran away while in kindergarten with a friend. In high school she threatened our parents all the time. As soon as she was out of school, she left home."

Amy shrugged, but Toby saw the sadness in his friend's eyes.

"I don't know why. She won't say. Just keeps moaning and crying over and over."

"Want me to talk with her?"

Doubt mingled with hope on her face, but doubt won out. "No, don't bother. I took some tea and crackers and insisted she lie down for a bit. Hopefully, she'll be more reasonable after awhile."

"I came over to ask you if you'd like to go with Andy and Caro to the fundraiser for kids in Huntington. Andy donated a painting and they're auctioning it off. Should bring in quite a bit. It's a big shindig, so we'll have to dress up."

"I'd love to, but—" She tilted her head in the direction of her office.

"Hmm. That is a problem." Toby scratched his head, thinking. "I'll tell you what. Ask her to go along too. Andy will have his SUV so there should be plenty of room, and he said he has plenty of extra tickets."

"I doubt she'll go, but I'll ask her. Give me an hour, and I'll call you and let you know. I hate to leave her like this."

Toby frowned. He wasn't used to Amy putting him off. Ever since they'd begun hanging together, she'd pretty much agreed to do whatever he asked, whether it was help with the town community plays or attend a function with him. It seemed odd that suddenly she was putting someone else ahead of him.

And he wasn't at all sure he liked it.

Chapter Twelve

Amy had to smile at Toby's suddenly disgruntled face. He was way too used to her giving in to his requests. Maybe she needed to play a little harder to get. Not too much. Just enough to force him to face the facts.

And just what are the facts, Amy Sanderson?

The question nagged at her as she returned to her office to check on her sister.

She loved him. A lot. That was a definite fact.

She'd allowed herself to be much too available to his whims and wishes. That was a definite.

That in spite of all her prayers, and hints to Toby, he still considered her *like a sister*. She didn't *like* it one little bit.

But what was she going to do about it? Maybe an extra-long prayer tonight reminding God that Toby was the one for her would help. Maybe.

Amy peeked into her office. Her sister looked sound asleep. She hoped so. Maybe a sound nap would put her in a better mood.

Jazzi had always been difficult, and they'd never been close. Even though they were only two years apart. It was as if Jazzi, the elder, resented the attention Amy got.

It wasn't as if Jazzi didn't get what she wanted. Even after all her rebelliousness, Amy knew—whether Jazzi did or not—their parents had equally divided their assets between them.

Her parents were good people, but way too busy with their work, then later with all the travels for work and pleasure. They were church members but rarely attended services. It was only after they'd moved to Appleton that Amy had found a church she'd fallen in love with—and friends that were real and great examples for her

She'd adored the Gibson brother and sister. The devotion they showed each other, their strength in pursuing their love of antiques and anything unusual, their sibling bond along with their teasing and squabbling that alarmed no one, least of all her. Their fighting was nothing like Jazzi and hers.

Caro's big heart had taken the lonely girl—herself—under her wing. From that moment on, her new friend had placed Amy front and center in Toby's view. For a long time, he'd ignored her and treated her like a child—if he even noticed her. Maybe that was the problem. She was too available.

But the last year, it'd been different. It was as if Toby had wakened from a dream and saw her as more than a child.

"Amy."

She turned from the window she stared through. Jazzi was awake, although she still lay on the loveseat.

"Jazzi. You're awake.

"Yeah."

"Do you feel better?"

A shrug was the only answer she got. Amy drew in a deep breath, trying to think of something to say to this sister-stranger in her office.

"Do you feel like talking?"

"No."

The word was terse, but Amy caught the tiniest lip tremor, and her suspicion was confirmed when Jazzi nipped at her bottom lip. The tears weren't very far from the surface.

"Toby was here a few minutes ago and asked us to go along with him, Andy and Caro to a society fundraiser in Huntington. Would you be interested? We'd have to put on our best gowns..."

"I didn't bring anything fancy with me."

"You have tons of clothes you left at Mom and Dad's—"

"No. I won't touch them."

"You can wear something of mine."

"I don't have an escort. You have Toby, and Caro and Andy are married. I won't go as a fifth wheel."

"Nonsense—"

"No. I mean it." Jazzi crossed her arms, and Amy couldn't stop the thought that her sister was acting like a spoiled five-year-old instead of a woman of twenty-ish.

Amy tapped her lips, thinking. If she could coax a certain someone to go along as Jazzi's escort, the problem would be solved.

"I'll tell you what. I have a friend—a handsome, tall, rugged guy who I know. I bet he'd love to go as your escort. And once he gets a load of you dressed up, there won't be any dissuading him. Shall I call him?"

"What's his name?" Her suspicious tone suggested she didn't trust Amy.

"Ryle. Ryle Sadler."

~*~

Toby had never been more surprised than

when they'd stopped at the apartment where Ryle lived and saw him coming down the sidewalk. Dressed to the nines in a tuxedo, Ryle was not the same man. This was not the helper who worked for Toby two or three days a week. This was not a laborer tonight.

"Wow. You clean up good." Toby leaned forward from the back seat where he sat and slapped Ryle on the back, once his friend had settled into the middle seat.

"I could say the same about you." Ryle tossed his amused remark back at his friend. "I do clean up—as you put it—now and then. In fact, I've been known to do it far more often than I like."

"Really? I think you and I need to have a talk."

"Not anytime soon, I hope." Ryle turned his back and stared at the window for the time it took to arrive at the huge house Andy was pulling up to.

"I'll go get the girls." Toby started to push up the seat to get out, but Ryle held up a hand.

"Allow me."

No one spoke as the three still in the vehicle watched the long-legged man stroll up the sidewalk and ring the doorbell. Toby chuckled at the man's gait. Ryle had told him when he'd first arrived in town that he'd always worked on a ranch out west, but had moved east to decide what he wanted to do with his life.

"Is that Jazzi?" Andy's voice was quiet and awed.

"Of course it is, Silly. How could you not recognize her with all that purple hair?" Caro chided her husband in a teasing tone.

Even with the purple hair and way too much eye makeup, Amy's sister was still stunning. Dressed in a soft pink long gown with the tiniest of sequins spreading around the neckline, it was the perfect color for the girl. And unlike her crying earlier today, there was a small smile on her face as she clutched Ryle's arm. Her eyes might still have a touch of redness about them, but it was so slight that few would notice.

"How did you get Ryle to agree to come? I've always tagged him as an outdoorsman." Toby studied the man who looked as at home in his tux as he did in his everyday work clothes.

"So he is." Caro half-turned in her seat. "I didn't ask him. Amy did, and he agreed willingly. I think she filled him in on her sister's mood. He really admires Amy and, I think, would do pretty much anything she'd ask."

Really? He sounded a mite too invested in Amy and her wishes.

Amy climbed in first and settled into the back seat beside him. Ryle helped Jazzi in then trotted to the other side and slid in beside her.

Toby heard Ryle's quiet whisper to Amy's sister. "Are you okay?"

When Jazzi nodded, his part-time employee smiled and nodded. "Good. I'm looking forward to seeing Andy's painting."

"How did you accomplish that?" Toby tilted his head in the direction of the middle seat.

"Easy. Ryle's always a good sport. Once I convinced Jazzi I had a handsome man lined up to escort her, she was eager to go." Amy glanced up at him, her eyes twinkling at him.

"Well, however you did it, your sister looks

stunning."

"I know. She's always been beautiful, but downplayed it to fit in with the crowd she ran with."

Was that a trace of wistfulness in her voice? He took a second glance at his partner-for-the-evening.

"Not any more beautiful than you. I've never seen anyone who looks as good in blue as you."

"Wow, Toby. That's the nicest thing I've ever heard you say to me."

Toby scrambled to back up. It wouldn't do to let her know his heart had picked up its pace as he watched her walk toward Andy's vehicle, the shimmering blue gown accenting her short, tiny body.

~*~

Toby stood just inside a recessed area where some kind of tall plant with enormous leaves held reign and watched his friends mingle with all the guests of the evening. Amy stood with Starli, Caro and Toni while Andy was being led around by someone Toby reckoned was the curator of the business. Jazzi and Ryle were in the reception room, still nibbling on all the hors d'oeuvre offered. This was an amazing display of how well Andy was being received in the art world. No doubt everything was too pricey for Toby's pocket, but he would give it all a glance-over anyway.

He slid into the reception room, and Ryle looked over at him and winked. So...he was handling the moody sister just fine. By the looks of it, she was having quite a time. He hoped Ryle was able to keep her in control.

An hour later, Amy and Toby hooked up again and headed to the room where the auction of Andy's painting was to be held. Passing the plant where he'd hidden earlier long enough to catch his breath, low voices caught his attention. Grabbing Amy's arm, he pulled her to the side and held up a finger to his lips.

"No. I'm done with you." Jazzi's voice bordered on panic. "You promised and promised but haven't carried through on anything."

A second voice remonstrated with her. "Come on, Jazz. You know I didn't mean half the stuff I said. Granddad had just finished chewing me out again. Besides, remember I told you if I can—"

"I don't care about all that and definitely don't care who your grandfather is."

"You didn't think that before. Has your sister—"

"Get away from me. Ouch—"

Toby was just ready to step forward to put a stop to the conversation when another voice interrupted.

"Jazzi, it's time for the auction. Coming?"

It was Ryle.

"What's wrong with your wrist? Has this— this man hurt you?"

Toby couldn't hear Jazzi's response but didn't have time to wonder about it. In an instant the other man fled the recessed area, shoving at him as he passed.

"Did you get a look at him?" Toby pulled Amy away from the area, not wanting to upset her sister or have her accuse them of spying.

"Not positive. Looked like Aaron, but the

dim light didn't help any." Amy tugged on his arm. "If we're going to watch the sale of Andy's painting, we need to go now."

Nodding, he followed her, only glancing back once to check on Ryle and Jazzi. But by the looks of things, his friend had everything under control.

~*~

"I'll get out here with Toby." Ryle slid out of Andy's car and Toby followed.

Good-byes said, Ryle stood on the side walk with Toby, his gaze roving the street in front of him.

"You want to talk, I assume."

It wasn't a question, and Toby hadn't meant it to be.

"Yeah. I'm afraid for Jazzi." The worried note in Ryle's voice proved the truth of his statement.

"Is she in trouble?"

Ryle hesitated. "I'm not sure. But that Aaron she came to town with—well, let's just say he's not to be trusted."

"Tell me more. How do you mean?" The man hadn't said much—ever—the few times he'd been around Toby, but there'd been something in his eyes Toby didn't like.

"I'm pretty sure, he's over-possessive of Jazzi. I can't pinpoint anything illegal he's done, but his vibes don't add up. The grip he had on her tonight was a little too much."

"So that was Aaron at the art gallery?"

"Yes. I'm not sure how he got in—"

"Looked like he was partially dressed up, as if serving as a waiter. Could be he conned his way in like that."

"I'd say you're right." Ryle shook his head. "She was really frightened tonight. We'd better keep an eye out for the guy. If he is the possessive type, he won't let go of her so easily."

"I think it's time for a little background check on the guy. Do you know his last name?"

"No. Maybe Amy can get it for us. I'll ask her tomorrow."

Why did Ryle automatically assume *he* was the one who should ask anything of Amy?

Toby unclenched his jaw. "Fine. And if we can find out what he does for a living, all the better."

"If. Not sure what he does is legit."

"Agreed. But the more we learn, the better we'll know how to deal with him. Or at the worst, can fill Detective Eddie in and let him send him out of town."

"He hasn't had to do that for a long time." Ryle laughed. "I'd better get home. See you tomorrow."

"Want me to run you home?"

"No. I need to clear my head. Haven't been to a doings like tonight for a couple years."

"Thanks for doing this for Amy. She appreciates it, you know, and so do I."

"My pleasure. Amy's a sweet girl. Who wouldn't want to make her happy?"

Toby watched Ryle stroll down the street in a wide-legged stride. Quietly confident completely described his friend. He wondered again what Ryle's history was. The man was allergic to talking about his past.

Turning to head to his apartment, Toby stopped to stare at Bloomin' Life. Ryle's affectionate tone when speaking of Amy was a little too much to suit Toby.

Had that been a subtle hint that Toby should be the one making her happy?

~*~

"Take your places." Toby called out the next afternoon at the theater. But when no lead romantic hero took the stage, his brows lifted. "Where's Jason?"

Krissy raised one shoulder. "He said he'd be late."

Toby drew in the deepest breath he could. If only he dared send the young man down the road talking to himself—but he couldn't. The rehearsals had gone on far too long to chance placing another person in the role. But how he'd love to.

"All right. Amy? Amy, where are you?"

"Here, Toby." She came from behind the stage left.

"Is Ryle here tonight?"

"No. He had plans tonight."

"Great." His mutter wasn't anywhere as gracious as it should have been. "Then I'll take the part to finish this scene till Jason gets here. Will you see if you can locate him and hustle him along, Amy?"

Amy nodded and hurried away from the stage.

"Okay, Krissy, let's start at the beginning of the scene. Ready?

The girl was a natural and a good choice for their play. She didn't have enough determination to go far, even if she had a vague desire to, but for their small local plays, she'd do.

They'd almost finished the scene before Jason strolled in, the smug grin on his face raising Toby's ire even higher. He raised his voice. "Take five, people."

With a forcefulness he usually didn't use, he approached Jason. "Couldn't you at least have the courtesy to call me if you're going to be late?"

"Didn't have time. I told Krissy to give you a heads up." The boy leaned against the wall and crossed his arms.

Toby studied the lad. He was good looking with decent—but not spectacular—talent, but the worst problem with him was his attitude. "Jason, I've already asked you several times to be here on time, know your lines and put yourself into the scenes. I know you can do it; you've shown me at times you can. I don't want to fire you."

Jason stared back at him, unblinking, defiant. "I don't mind. Do it."

If only—

"Toby, we've got a problem."

Amy's low whisper bordered on panic.

"What is it?"

"Come with me."

Turning back to Jason, he motioned. "Go get a drink and find Krissy. We'll begin again in a few minutes. Be ready."

He turned to Amy. "What's going on?"

"More damages. Remember when we thought someone had searched our props room?"

"Not again."

"Worse. They destroyed that old settee we use quite often in our plays."

It was worse than Amy had explained. Not

only was the settee torn, the stuffing flung in abandon, but two locked doors were destroyed with what could only have been an ax. Items had been swept from the shelves, as if a hand had knocked them over for spite.

Nothing was of any value and could be replaced. But the time to gather what they'd lost would be precious hours away from his work and the play. He'd just have to gather the pieces as needed.

"What's going on, Toby? Who hates you enough to do this?"

For the first time, Amy's eyes showed fear.

~*~

Amy slipped her hand in Toby's as they walked toward The Coffee House. It'd been a stressful evening, especially for this man beside her. He was such a good person. Strong. Talented. Determined. Gentle. And he must have the patience of a slow moving turtle to put up with his two leading actors.

He'd not said a lot, but he didn't have to. His face had said enough, and it'd broken her heart.

Not that the items lost couldn't be replaced. They could, and Toby would, but it was the act itself that was so disturbing. Someone destroying what Toby and the community had worked so hard to do... Providing clean, wholesome entertainment for his friends, neighbors and fellow-Appleton-citizens. Why?

She kept pace with his slow steps, burdened with trying to figure it all out.

"I want it back."

For a moment Amy thought Toby was growling in a deep, rough voice for some reason, and then it hit her...

Someone behind them was speaking to Toby. Or her.

They turned slowly, and as they did, Toby stepped to the right, placing her a few steps behind him.

A figure in dark clothes, a ball cap pulled low over his face faced them. And in his hands was a gun.

Pointed at Toby.

~*~

In a ridiculous moment of playback, Toby thought of the fear playing across Amy's face at the theater. Now, all he could feel was a very real fear. Not so much that he'd be killed. Or Amy. No. But the fear of not knowing what on earth was going on. Why couldn't he get some tangible evidence to point him in the direction of why he was suddenly the target of an unknown criminal?

"What do you want? If you'd only tell me—"

"Shut up."

"Let's talk this out. No need for dramatics."

"I want you to keep walking. Answer my questions, and you won't get hurt. Or your girl."

"If I knew what you wanted, I'd be glad to help you find what you want."

"I said, shut up. I'll ask the questions. If you know what's good for you, you'll walk easy. I've used this gun before and won't hesitate to use it again."

Toby nodded, figuring he'd pushed him as far as he should. Turning slowly, he motioned to Amy to walk.

"Where did you hide it?"

"What do you think I hid? You've been in my

shop. I hid nothing." Well, except for Caro's treasure chest, which the guy happened to find. "Everything I have there is for sale."

"Grand—we know you have it. Someone saw you loading it up at the auction."

"Saw me loading what? Listen, man, you're making no sense. If you give me the details, I can help you. Otherwise, this is hopeless."

"I can't say anymore. It's a—a—I'm bound to not say too much."

That could mean only one thing. Whatever this "thing" was, it was sinister. *How* it was sinister was yet to be discovered.

"What's your name?"

"Yeah, I'm about to tell you." Was that a crack in the man's voice? Defensive, definitely, and the sarcasm and trace of anger told Toby more than anything else that this guy was desperate.

Maybe it was time to take the initiative. Maybe the guy wasn't as tough as he thought.

"Listen—" Toby whirled, leaped and grabbed at the gun. But he wasn't quite quick enough. With a jerk, the man struck out at Toby, grazing the side of his head, and ran, faster than Toby'd ever seen someone run before. Toby staggered and fell against the side of the brick building.

Amy came up alongside him. "Toby, are you okay?"

Toby lifted a hand and touched the bleeding gash on his head. "Yeah, I'm fine. Stunned me for a second there."

"But you're bleeding."

"It's nothing."

"What did you think you were doing? The

man held a gun." Amy's indignant voice scolded even though a worried thread wove through it.

"He wasn't going to shoot us. He was scared."

"How on earth could you know that?" If anything, the indignation grew stronger.

"His voice."

"Uh huh. All I heard was 'I have a gun and not afraid to use it.'"

"Yeah, he did say that."

"Is that all you've got to say?"

Would little Amy be as peeved at him if she knew what he suspected?

A short whine of a siren sounded, and Toby glanced at Amy again. "You called the cops?"

"Someone has to think straight." She scolded, but the tears in her eyes told him how scared she'd been.

A black and white patrol car pulled up alongside the curb. A window slid down, and Detective Eddie's long, sad-looking face peered at them.

"Are you two all right? What did you do to make Amy dock you one, Toby Gibson?"

"I didn't."

"She didn't." At least they agreed on something.

"Well, that explains everything. Jump in, and you can fill me in on the details of what Amy didn't do."

The detective's tone was dry, but Toby knew that their town cop was the smartest, most gentle, but firmest, guy around. There wasn't anything he wouldn't do for the citizens of Appleton. He cared about them, and his work showed it.

"There's not much definitive information to tell." Toby shrugged.

"Toby, did you ever call Detective Eddie and tell him about the break-ins?

Was that an accusatory tone in Amy's voice?

"I was going to." Toby made sure his tone was quite insistent. Just in case either of them had any doubts about his action.

"But you didn't."

"If you two love-birds will quit your fussing at each other and tell me what's going on, I'd appreciate it." Detective Eddie's sour tone was deceiving.

"I really was going to call you, but with the play's opening night beelining toward us faster than a jet plane, and, well, everything else, I didn't get it done."

"Okay, so tell me now, what about the break-ins?"

"It started over a month ago with someone breaking into Undiscovered Treasures in the middle of the night. At first I thought it was just creaks and groans of an older building, then I realized someone was downstairs looking around."

"Really, Toby. You should have called me. How many times did this happen?"

No doubt about it. Detective Eddie was peeved at him. "Three."

"Four, counting the damage to the van," Amy corrected him.

"Right."

"Was anything stolen?" Detective Eddie snapped the question at them.

"No—"

"Yes, the treasure chest."

"I was going to say that."

"But you didn't."

Toby sighed. "At first, nothing was taken although I noticed faint disturbances, but nothing that set my alarm on panic."

"He joked about it being a *ghost*. Can you believe that?"

If the tears in her voice was anything to go on, Amy was still upset.

"And that's all it was. A joke."

"And finally this *ghost* did steal."

"Yes, but first he broke the window of my van, then he destroyed Amy's greenhouse."

Detective Eddie turned in his seat to stare at her. "And you didn't think to call me?"

"Well, I..."

"Uh huh. Don't make excuses. You're just as bad as this scoundrel in my front seat." The man rebuked her but in a much softer tone. "You could have both been hurt."

"But we weren't."

"Yeah, I see that." And the man stared at Toby's head.

Toby touched the wound again. The bleeding had stopped, but the pounding had gotten worse.

"You've got five minutes to complete the story, then I suggest you head to the emergency room and let someone look at that. Might be more serious than you think."

It was the slowest five minutes in his life as Toby—with Amy's input—finished their story.

In spite of his protest, Amy insisted, with Detective Eddie's backing, that the emergency room check out the wound on his head. Reluctantly, he gave in.

Now, he scowled as the Doctor reported,

after an ex-ray, he had a mild concussion and recommended an overnight stay for him.

He would have protested had it not been for the pleading in Amy's eyes and the warning in Detective Eddie's. He didn't want to see hurt replacing the pleading in Amy's eyes, nor go against that warning in Appleton's police chief's.

He was only too glad to finally be alone as Detective Eddie led Amy away an hour later. Amy's orders to behave and rest, that Ryle and she would take care of everything, didn't do much to reassure him.

He settled his head against the overly-plump pillow. It was time to figure out who this mysterious trespasser was. If his guess was right, it could only be one of two people.

But that last thought said it all: a guess, which meant he could possibly be wrong.

Or right.

One thing he did know. He wasn't about to share his suspicions of the man who'd held a gun pointed at them tonight. Especially with Amy.

Chapter Thirteen

A week later

Toby and Ryle headed for one of the estate auctions his friend had told him about. Though most times, Ryle drove, today, Toby had insisted. That one-night stand at the hospital had turned to three when the doctor wasn't as pleased with his concussion improvement as he wished. Toby had been chomping at the bit to get away, and this auction had been a good excuse. With Caro back in the store, he had no worries—today.

Too many things were happening. In less than a month now, Appleton's Spring Fest would begin. The play rehearsals should have been headed down the final weeks of preparation. Instead, here he was still holding his breath every evening before rehearsal, wondering if his lead actors would show up.

He should have known better than to cast two romantically involved young people together in important roles. He should have, but he hadn't. Their casting had pushed them further ahead of any others who'd auditioned for the roles. At the time, he'd been sure his choice was the right one. Too bad he hadn't realized then what trouble was in store in just a few weeks.

Toby glanced over at his companion for the day. Two hours into the drive, and Ryle had said little since they'd climbed into the van and headed out for the auction over near

Morgantown. If the frown marring his friend's forehead was any sign, then the man had worries as bad as Toby's...or maybe worse.

"You okay?"

Ryle's brow cleared. "Yeah. Just keeping an eye on the black and silver car behind us."

"Where?" Giving the mirror a sharp glance, he studied the line of cars behind them. "Are you sure?"

"Pretty much so. Only one of those four cars has stayed on the same route we're taking. A three hour drive? Seems a little strange."

"Hmm. I should think. I don't see it."

"Oh, the driver's good. Doesn't get too close. Keeps a vehicle between us or if there isn't any, he hangs back too far to make out the license plate."

"Thinks he's smart, does he?" Toby grinned. "Let's try something."

"Such as?"

"Such as finding the right side road to turn onto and hiding until it passes. Then we'll turn around and follow him."

"Shades of the wild, wild west. Might work. Let's give it a try."

"Keep your eyes peeled."

"You got it."

They drove for five minutes before both of them pointed at the same time. A road on the right turned off, but went immediately down a small slope, which would effectively hide the van for a few minutes. By the time the other vehicle realized the van was nowhere around, they'd be on their follower's tail.

Hopefully.

Neither spoke as Toby took the sharp right

and flew over the hill. There was enough room to pull over and maneuver until the van was again turned toward the main road.

"Another minute..." Ryle was gazing at his watch. "Five, four, three, two—go!"

Toby hit the gas, and the trusty old van did its best to pick up speed. As they topped the hill again and turned onto the highway, both men searched the main road. There, just heading around the next bend, was the long black car. Toby stomped the gas, and the van cooperated.

"What do you think? Close or hang back?" Toby didn't take his eyes off the car they were approaching.

"If we're going to do this, might as well go all the way. Close as you can get without causing an accident."

"When do you think they'll realize they've been spotted?"

"You'll know."

Sure enough, it wasn't a minute later that the car picked up speed, then slowed and turned off onto an exit. Toby cast a questioning glance at Ryle, but the man shook his head.

"Let 'em go. If they're serious, they'll pick up our trail again. They might even have placed a bug on the van to keep track of us."

"You think so?"

It was Ryle's turn to grin. "Not really. But whoever it is has probably done his homework. They'll know what the van is used for. Whatever the reason they're following us, they probably have guessed where we're going too."

"You know what that means?"

"Sure. They haven't found what they're after."

"I just can't figure out what that is or why they just don't ask for it."

"Who knows? But you'll know soon enough. They can't keep this up without getting recognized, and when you do, let Detective Eddie know. He'll take care of it. Pretty possessive of Appleton's citizens, he is."

"He is, isn't he? But he has a good heart."

An hour later, they turned into the driveway of the auction site. Old Mr. Cowell's figure walked with dignity and self-importance with each step—his cane tapping on the sidewalk—toward the auction house. Toby glanced at Ryle, then drove through the parking area looking for a good spot. He tapped the brakes and stared as the chauffeur of the black and silver car pulled into a spot.

~*~

"Here's what I want you to do, Ryle." Toby pulled Ryle to the side as they entered the huge building housing the items to be sold. "While I'm bidding, I want you to stick like glue to Barnabas Cowell and watch his every move."

"Like?"

"Who he talks with, what he bids on, where he goes." Toby grinned. "That should pretty well cover it, I'd think."

"Do you really think he's your trespasser? Not meaning any disrespect, but that old man?"

"No, I don't think he's my trespasser. But that doesn't mean he isn't behind all these happenings. And if he isn't, I mean to find out who is."

"Got it. I'll be his Super Glue today. Can't get rid of that very easily," Ryle joked as he walked away.

Toby chuckled. That didn't happen often—Ryle joking—but it was good to hear. The man had always been good with anything Toby had asked of him. He had no fears he wouldn't or couldn't follow through on this. At least, he could rest easy while he did his best to outbid others on the items he wanted.

As it happened, there were several pieces Toby was interested in. Two high-backed, brocaded antique chairs that Toby suspected would bring in good prices, another bedroom set—not even close to the set he'd wanted when Amy had outbid him weeks earlier—that would serve the purpose until he could find better, and surprise!—a chest, bigger and better than the one stolen from his shop.

He didn't even mind that he lost a bid on a maple, drop-leaf table, he was so pleased with his other purchases.

Once the auction was over, Toby paid for his purchases and looked around for Ryle. He'd been so excited, he'd forgotten about Ryle *and* Barnabas Cowell. But searching for twenty minutes and not finding his friend convinced him that he'd better find someone else to help him load the items he'd bought. Fortunately, there were men for hire to do the heavy lifting bidders didn't want to do, and Toby hired two of the stout men. He hurriedly explained what needed to be done, then began his search again for Ryle.

What to do? Was Ryle in trouble or had he had to follow a lead with no time to let Toby know? That made no sense. He had his cell so why wouldn't he call? But maybe he hadn't been able to. Maybe he'd been in trouble.

No, none of that made sense.

Unless he was hurt. But surely Barnabas Cowell wouldn't be able to do that. His chauffeur maybe, but not him. Hadn't he heard there were rumors about that family?

What if Ryle was involved? He still wasn't sure that the man running away in the building between his and Amy's businesses wasn't Ryle. He hoped not. He should have just asked, but then Ryle would know Toby had questions, and how would that be for their working relationship?

Calm down, he told himself. First things first. Check to see if Cowell's car was still in the parking lot, and if not...?

Toby hurried toward the lot, trying not to think of his next move. If only Detective Eddie was here. For once in his life, he'd like to have the man in charge. With him. Assuring him that Ryle was all right. That there was nothing to worry about.

But Detective Eddie wasn't here, and it would take him close to three hours to come, even if he would. He hated to call in cops he didn't know, but it might come to that.

Sighing, Toby set out to search the auction property one more time.

~*~

"Toby?"

Even before Toby turned, he knew the voice. "Sharlene? What are you doing here?"

Her laugh was short and full of amusement. "Business. Had to meet a—client."

"Here? At the auction?"

"Believe it or not."

She laughed again, but was it a bit forced?

Whatever the reason, right now, Toby couldn't care less. "A client refusing to pay what he bid on? That could cause a problem."

"I wish. Just an annoying client—excuse me for complaining—that thinks I have nothing better to do than to manage every unpleasant situation he manages to put himself into."

"Sounds quite the discouraging problem."

"Don't I know it?" Sharlene straightened as if pushing the topic away. "Were you able to outbid on the items you wanted?"

"Quite a few lovely pieces."

"Antique? I love antiques. May I see them?"

She was so suddenly filled with enthusiasm, Toby hated to say no. He'd searched every speck of the property and found not a clue on Ryle's disappearance. Nothing to do, but call the cops, and if Ryle didn't show up by the time his furniture was loaded, he'd do just that.

In the meantime...

"Sure. Follow me."

"I'd prefer to walk with you." She reached for his arm to slow him down. "What's the hurry?"

Toby stopped walking and glanced at her. "Am I hurrying?"

He wasn't about to tell her about Ryle. Why he wouldn't, wasn't entirely clear to him, unless it was that meeting between Sharlene and that Gordon man who'd taken Amy out for dinner. That didn't set quite right with him.

"You were about to."

"Okay. We'll take it nice and slow then." Even though he wanted to run.

Minutes later, they walked up to the loading dock. The two men who Toby had hired to load his purchases were nowhere to be seen. Worse, the van was gone.

"My van's gone." Toby wanted to groan. Instead, he pulled out his cell and dialed.

Sharlene laid a hand on his hand. "Wait. Are you sure you need to involve the police?"

Why would she automatically decide he was calling them?

"Who else should I call? I have a man, a van and some purchased items, all missing. Am I supposed to wait around till they all come home, wagging their tails behind them?" He was more frustrated than he usually felt, but this was bizarre. There was no getting around it.

If only he hadn't left the keys in the van. But it was *West Virginia*, and in Appleton, it was a normal habit. Obviously, he needed to remember that outside of there, removal of car keys was a necessity.

Turning his back to her, he finished dialing and when a dispatcher answered, he explained the problem. When she assured him an officer would be right there, he hung up and turned back to Sharlene.

She was gone.

~*~

By the time the police arrived, Toby was ready to change his mind again and call Detective Eddie. Another half hour passed with no new details. Only a promise from the police—that they would do all they could to find his friend and missing van. If and/or when his items were found, they couldn't assure him they wouldn't be damaged, or worse, sold.

So much for that. He was ready to call Amy,

when his cell rang. He answered it.

"Hello."

"Toby? It's Ryle." His whispering voice was filled with caution.

"Ryle, where are you?"

"I sneaked into the van when those two hoodlums you hired weren't looking. Have no idea yet where we are, but by the sounds of it, they've reached their destination. Gotta go. I'll give you a call back when I—"

"Hey, what are you doing back there? The boss isn't gonna like—" A gruff, coarse voice interrupted Ryle's explanation.

The phone went dead, and Toby stared down at it.

Where was Ryle?

What had just happened?

Toby dialed his cell again, and when the person on the other end answered, he said, "Detective Eddie, I need you."

~*~

"You must have used your siren all the way."

It'd been close to two and a half hours since Toby had called Detective Eddie.

"Sure did. Just remember, I've come in an unofficial capacity. Can't tread on another city's territory. But I know some tricks I'm sure none of these city cops have learned. Just don't tell them I said that. And I brought little Amy. Figured she could cheer you up a mite."

He'd already received and appreciated the hug she'd given him. It'd done worlds for his morale, but he wasn't about to voice it to anyone.

"Thanks, you two, for coming."

"Okay, let me go over and speak to the man

in charge and get the okay with me being here, then you can show me around the place a bit."

"Sure thing. We're not going anywhere." Toby might be hoping for more than the detective could produce, but if he had to choose anyone to help out in this scrape, it was Appleton's chief of police. Toby would bet his store on him, if he were a betting man.

Ten minutes later, Detective Eddie returned. He didn't report on the conversation he had with the Morgantown police, but he did ask for Toby to show him where the van had parked for loading and a rundown on what had happened.

"This is where the van was parked?" Detective Eddie squinted as he studied the area. "And Ryle was with it the whole time?"

"No. I asked him to keep an eye on something else for me while I was bidding."

Detective Eddie's gaze sharpened. "And what was this something else?"

"A person, but I don't think an old man could have stolen the van. He rides in a chauffeured car. Somehow I can't see him stealing an old van."

"I see." Detective Eddie walked slowly around the area, his gaze on the ground, but occasionally taking in the near area. "Hmm."

He squatted once and touched the pavement with a finger, then lifted it to his nose and sniffed. Nodding, he stood again.

Five minutes later, he motioned to Amy and Toby. "Jump in if you're going." He strode to his police car and climbed in, not waiting to see if they followed.

Amy and Toby hurried to follow. Toby asked

as he buckled his seat belt, "Did you find a clue?"

"Yes," was the terse reply.

Toby grabbed the dash as the detective spun out of the parking lot, but once back on the main road, he slowed, sped up, and slowed down again.

"Did you find a clue back there, Detective Eddie?" Amy coaxed.

Toby knew she hoped to get an answer.

"You could say that," He snapped. "Keep your eyes peeled."

The man drove in starts and stops, and once, he pulled half-way off the county road to jump out of the car and inspect something. When he returned to his seat, he was grinning like he'd won the lottery.

"You do have a clue." Toby was sure of it, but whether Detective Eddie would share what it was, was another matter.

"Your van has a small oil leak, but enough I can follow. We're getting close. I figure we'll be turning onto a back road anytime now." He didn't take his eyes off the road. "And...here it is."

With a sudden move, he turned right onto a narrow, dirt road, grass growing in spots on it.

~*~

This was the most exciting thing that had happened in her life for a long time. Of course, the destruction at Bloomin' Life had been shocking, but no way exciting. And knowing Detective Eddie had asked her to participate, even if it was as a move to keep Toby calm, was a nice touch. But the icing on the cake had been Toby's tight clutch when Amy had hugged him. He hadn't said much, but the hug had done the talking.

Amy gazed out the windows of the vehicle. The overlapping branches of the tall trees shut out most of the sunlight on what was a beautiful spring day. The effect gave the driveway an eerie feeling, and Amy felt the chill bumps creep up her spine. Where would this deserted-looking road lead? Did Detective Eddie really know where he was going, or was it a wild guess?

Toby hadn't said much the last few miles. Worried, Amy was sure. If they did find the van, would it be destroyed? The items inside damaged? And worse, would Ryle be okay? Her heart pounded harder at the thought of that young man hurt or...no, she wouldn't think that.

She clutched the armrest and breathed a prayer.

~*~

Detective Eddie crept around a bend and stopped abruptly. Ahead, a hundred feet or so, stood a dilapidated house, the surrounding area filled with junk of all kinds. Most important of all was Toby's van, parked close to a porch that looked as if it was about to fall down.

Toby grasped the door handle, ready to jump out.

"Wait." Detective Eddie's hand on his arm stopped him. "Give it a minute or so. Then I'm going to get out. Toby, you follow me, but stay close behind me. Amy, stay in the car, and by no means get out. If something bad—if something happens to us, use the radio and call for help. Then you get in that driver's seat and get out of here as fast as you can."

"I'm not leaving you two."

Amy was scared, Toby could tell, but the fierce determination not to abandon them ran strong through her words.

Detective Eddie lowered his head and gave her a stern look. "You can help us best by not allowing me to worry about you. Can you do that?"

Amy drew in a deep breath. "I can, but I don't want to leave without you."

"I doubt you'll have to. I'm fairly savvy, you know." And the man's grin was back in place.

Following the detective's lead, Toby exited the vehicle and stayed close behind. He didn't go in a straight line, but followed the trail of junk in the yard, moving from one large item to another. They approached the van, and Detective Eddie held up a hand. For a long minute, he listened, then moved to the passenger door and peered through a window.

"Empty," he mouthed the word. Moving to the back of the van, he peeked in the back door windows. Shaking his head, he pulled out his gun, and motioning to Toby to open the doors, he leveled his gun.

Toby gripped the door handles, drew in a slow breath, and flung them open.

Inside the van, behind the pieces of furniture, two feet stuck out.

Toby stared at the feet, then with a bound, he was in the van. He shoved the two chairs out of the way and looked down at the figure leaning against the side of the van, eyes closed, head sunk to his chest. Kneeling, Toby patted Ryle's pale face and checked his pulse.

"He's alive." He leaned back to see around

the chest. "Can you motion for Amy to join us so she can take care of Ryle while I help you?"

"Got it." The detective stepped out of the van and motioned to Amy.

"She coming?" Toby glanced at the man again.

"On her way. Not sure I need your help." Detective Eddie swiveled his gaze from the house and back to Toby. "Do we need an ambulance?"

"I don't think so, but he should be checked out. Looks like he was knocked out. There's a slight bump on his head."

"Let me watch over him." It was Amy, climbing up into the van. "You go with Detective Eddie. I'll see if I can make Ryle more comfortable and call an ambulance."

The two men stalked across the remainder of the lawn—if it could be called that. Detective Eddie motioned to Toby to head around back. "Careful," he whispered.

It was over in a matter of minutes. When Detective Eddie crashed through the front door, Toby slammed through the back. Both of the hired men were lounging at a table, playing cards, bottles of liquor scattered about the room. Neither gave them any resistance as Detective Eddie held out handcuffs for Toby to cuff them. Their only protest was that they were only following orders.

"Whose orders?" Toby's demand was accompanied with a slight shake.

"No idea," The smaller man whined.

"Shut up." The bigger one was obviously the leader. "We don't know nothing. A guy approached us and told us 'plans were changed.' We were to take the van and possessions away for a mite of time. They'd be in touch."

"What did this man look like?"

"Tall. Thin. Don't know nothing else. Didn't ask no name."

Toby glanced at Detective Eddie who shook his head. "No need to pressure them right now. I'll haul them into the station. Think I hear the sirens. It'll be the ambulance. You and Amy take care of Ryle and report back to me later tonight. Okay?"

"Sure." Toby hesitated long enough to stroll through the house again. Scattered bottles, food-encrusted plates piled in the sink, and a general disarray cluttered the disheveled place. But in the corner, Toby saw something that made him stoop to examine.

The missing chest from his garage. The lock had been smashed, a few of the items scattered around the chest, but since nothing of immense value had been stored in it, and the chest was damaged beyond repair, Toby left it.

Following Detective Eddie out the door and back to the cruiser, he hailed him and explained what he'd found. The man shook his head and offered to get it for evidence if nothing else against the two men.

As Detective Eddie left with his two criminals and the chest, the ambulance pulled in, and Toby motioned them over to the van. As they unloaded the equipment they needed, Toby headed to the front of the van to make sure it would start. Satisfied, it should take him back as far as civilization before needing road assistance, Toby jumped out and slammed the door shut.

Amy joined him as the paramedics took over with Ryle and lifted him into the ambulance.

"I want to go with them to make sure Ryle is all right." Amy brushed away the strands of hair against her cheekbones.

"I understand. Go. I'll be right behind you and will check on you both later, maybe around nine."

As the ambulance left, Toby headed to the van. Hopefully, the thieves of his van hadn't damaged it, and the van would get him home. Otherwise he'd have a long wait before he'd see the lights of Appleton.

Chapter Fourteen

It was closer to ten before Toby was able to get to the hospital.

The van had gotten him back to Appleton all right, but given up the ghost as they entered the town limit. By the time the tow truck arrived to haul it to the service garage Toby normally hired for repairs, it was an hour past the time he'd promised Amy.

When he entered Ryle's room, Amy was curled up in the chair nearby the bed, her eyes closed.

The nurse outside had assured him Ryle should be all right and probably wake up in the next few hours. So Toby hauled the next available chair close to the bed and settled into it to wait till one or both of his friends wakened.

Amy stirred and opened her eyes. Giving him a big smile, she stretched. "I needed that nap. Have you talked with Detective Eddie?"

"On the phone, but he hasn't had time to question the men yet. Had a disturbance across town and went out again to handle that. You?"

"About Ryle. Doctor said he thought he'd be all right. They'll let him go home after he rouses." Amy checked her watch. "Should be anytime now."

"Want to go over what we know?"

"Do we know anything?"

"Not much, but talking it over might give us

172

some ideas."

"Shoot then."

"First, I had four break-ins at Undiscovered Treasures. You had one at your shop, and that was after my four."

"Meaning?"

"Meaning after searching my place, they didn't find what they were looking for and moved on to yours."

"Sounds about right. But why search our places at all?"

"I'm thinking somehow the auctions are key to the mystery. How else could it work? I mean, auctions are the main source of supply for my shop, hence I frequent them, and you too occasionally."

"That makes sense. But how do we know *they* do?"

"I don't know the answer to that yet. But I think we can figure out what set them on the search."

"Quick. Tell me."

"First, it sounds reasonable to think someone lost something valuable. Why else would they be so desperate as to commit a crime?"

"Or it could be they are professional thieves after a valuable thing."

"That's true. Somehow they've targeted my place. Why? I think they suspect it—whatever *it* is—was sold at an auction."

"Auction?" Amy's eyes grew thoughtful. "Because they know the person who put it up for sale."

"Or they accidentally sold it, not realizing the value."

"Then it couldn't be an antique because why sell it if they now want it back?"

"Hmm. I think you're right." Toby rubbed a hand over his short-cut hair. "Then perhaps a relative sold it, not realizing how valuable it was."

"Maybe it was found, or gifted or inherited."

"And maybe that person didn't like or want the thing."

"Or didn't like antiques."

"Too many ifs. Let's move on." No use rambling around with useless ideas. "Back to what we do know—or at least, what we can guess about and be confident we have a chance of being close."

"What is that?"

"While driving home this afternoon, I thought back over what has happened in the last month or so. First, there are some new people in town, and so far, *I* know little about why they're here."

"You're talking about Gordon Rickward and Glamour Girl what's-her-name."

"Sharlene Miller, yes. Do you have any ideas why *he's* here?"

"Said he'd heard about our town and wanted to take a few days leave to visit."

"Did he sound legit when he said that?"

"I think so. He was flirting, so I took some things he said with a grain of salt."

"Flirting?" Toby growled the question.

Amy waved a hand. "Meant nothing to me, and especially after I saw him and your Sharlene kissing."

"Oh, yeah, that. And she's not my Sharlene."

"And he means nothing to me." Her voice

was as emphatic as his.

"Okay. We've settled that. So what about them?"

"Sharlene said she was here working for a client. Have no clue who the client is."

"Anyway we can find out?"

"We could follow them."

"Now that might be interesting."

"Or boring. Dangerous. Embarrassing." Toby put as much warning into his voice as possible.

"But we might get answers."

"There might be an easier way."

"Such as?

"We could ask Detective Eddie to do some background checks—discreetly, of course—on those two. Who knows? He might be able to find out who Sharlene's clients are."

"Do you think he'd do it?" Amy whispered her question.

"We'll never know unless we ask. I think that should be your job."

"Mine? Why me?"

"Who do you think he'd be more apt to say yes to?" He was being clever by pinpointing her like that, but it was the truth. Detective Eddie, as tough as he was, hardly ever said no to a female.

"All right, I'll do it." Her agreement wasn't especially pleasant, but reluctant. "Is there anyone else we should be thinking about?"

"Definitely. What about that sour Cowell man? He's totally antagonistic. He showed up at two of the same auctions where I went. And he argued with me over a piece of furniture I'd already sold."

"Could be he just likes antiques."

"I think he mentioned that. But there's also this: he was at the auction today. In fact, he's the one I asked Ryle to watch while the auction was going on."

"Really? And Ryle's never been able to tell you what, if anything, has happened since then."

"No. I'm looking forward to finding out what he says."

"I just thought of something. There are two others we should keep our eyes on." Amy straightened her shirt, her eyes lowered.

"Who?"

"Jazzi and that Aaron guy."

"I can't see Jazzi doing this. Not sure about Aaron after seeing how he talked to Jazzi at Andy's art sale."

"I can. She's always been pretty wild, Toby. You don't know her."

"But she's your sister."

"Yes, she is." Amy said nothing more, only shook her head.

"Well, we can ask Detective Eddie to ask about Aaron too. Do you think you can find out his last name?"

"I think so."

"Good. I still have no idea what it is someone is searching for, so let's move on to what and make some guesses."

"You said Mr. Cowell wanted furniture. Do you suppose something valuable could be hidden in one of them?"

"Not in any I have on hand. Maybe something I've already sold. But what about this? Why did the person break into Bloomin' Life? And tear up the greenhouse, of all things?

If he or she thought something was there, then it would have to be small. Couldn't be an art picture. Wouldn't stand being unprotected in the dirt."

"Jewels? I've heard of thieves hiding them in dirt till they have a clear path to get them out."

"That's a good thought. But we found none. And I looked pretty good."

"There's that. I don't think we can guess what it is without more to go on."

"It's confusing. My business and yours? Too different."

"Yeah, I know. This is hopeless."

"Don't give up yet. I'm planning on contacting Sharlene."

"What for?"

Toby had never heard Amy's voice before with that much suspicion in it. Or was it jealousy?

"For a date, of course."

~*~

It was the next evening, but Ryle still hadn't wakened, and the nurses had urged both of them to go home and get some rest. They assured Amy and Toby they'd be the first called when he did waken. Both had reluctantly agreed.

Amy had been enthusiastic about Toby's plan when he'd explained what he intended. Going on a date with Sharlene was only the beginning, providing she would even agree to such a thing. Could be she'd be too busy, or not even in town or maybe uninterested. In any of those cases, she'd just say no, probably in a nice way, but still a no.

But he didn't care. What he really wanted

was to find out who her client was, or anything else pertinent to finding out information about her.

The sun had barely risen when Amy had contacted Detective Eddie about Sharlene and Gordon—who reluctantly, and only after she'd explained in depth what was going on and why they wanted to know—agreed to get in touch with a contact who could give them some answers. That was taken care of. What bothered Toby was Amy's insistence on doing the same as him. She'd contact Gordon for a lunch date and see what would happen. She'd assured him she'd be fine.

And she no doubt would be, but that nth of a degree worried him. If Gordon was involved in something shady, then Amy could be in danger.

Toby hadn't mentioned the questions he had about Ryle. Fortunately, there was more than one tall, thin man in town—particularly Gordon and Aaron whatever-his-name-was. And if Gordon wore athletic shoes, he'd never wear cheap ones. As for Aaron—he wasn't so sure. But Ryle? He wore only the best.

As for Sharlene, he had her number on his cell, but he would like to know where she was staying. If she refused a date, he was going to locate her temporary housing, follow her for a few days and see if she was up to anything fishy.

Since there were no hotels in town—only a small bed and breakfast—he'd assumed Sharlene had a room there. When he called, the desk clerk assured him no one with the name of Sharlene Miller was staying there or ever had.

Ending the call, he pondered where else she could be staying. Out of town, perhaps Huntington or Charleston? Could be, but that was a forty-minute drive. So who did she know in town where she could stay?

Her client.

And that—he knew—was his primary purpose right now. If he found out who that was, then he could either eliminate her or...

It might just lead to an even bigger clue.

~*~

"What are we planning for Toby's birthday?" Amy and Caro were having lunch at The Coffee House.

"Nothing?" Caro swallowed her bite of the Italian sub on her plate.

"I can see that happening." Anyone who didn't know the Gibson brother and sister would think they did not get along. But Amy knew how close they were and with all their denials of it, their sibling teasings was just that. "Not."

"Do you have something in mind?"

"Well, we've done so many intellectual things lately, and Toby loves running. Why don't we do something more casual? We know he loves his work with the youth at church and the community theater he organizes and directs, so let's have a 5K and have all donations go to one of those two things he does. Or split the profit for both. Afterwards we can have a community picnic in the park."

Caro laid her sandwich back on her plate. "Amy, I think you might have just hit the jackpot. That is so totally perfect for Toby. But how are we going to pull this off without him hearing about it?"

"We're not. We can broadcast the event, but keep it from him that the donations will go to his two loves."

"Brilliant. Appleton citizens are pretty good at keeping secrets when necessary. I think it will work. fill in Starli and Toni on your idea, and they can help us organize it. What are you thinking? Right after the Fest or give it some time? Ha. Toby will think we've forgotten him."

"So much of a better surprise when it happens."

"And maybe I can skip out of buying him a birthday present with all our hard work in pulling this off successfully." Caro winked and snickered."

"Yeah, right. As if you'd do that. I already have his gift from me."

"Tell me." Caro leaned forward.

"Nope. It will be a surprise, but it's something he's wanted for a long time. We kind of had an argument over it."

"An argument?"

"Yep. But that's all I'm telling you. You'll have to wait."

"You don't trust me."

But the sly look in Caro's eyes told Amy the truth. Her friend wanted to know, and she'd do anything to find out the answer

~*~

It'd been a busy day. Amy had hated to leave Ryle this morning, but what the nurses said made sense, and she knew Toby wouldn't leave if she didn't. First thing tomorrow she'd head back to the hospital to check on their friend.

How could Gordon Rickward be connected

to hers and Toby's problems? Yet to be thorough, and to satisfy Toby, she was going to do this. And that meant keeping track of Gordon's movements, whether that meant a date or spying on him. He just didn't seem to be the type to be a thief. But what did she know about thieves?

Was it too late to call Gordon now? A quick glance at her bedside clock assured her she could probably squeeze by with calling him now. She lifted her cell and dialed his number, and when he answered—not a sleepy note in his voice—she explained her request and grinned when he gave her an enthusiastic yes.

Readying for bed, Amy smiled as she thought about Toby. He didn't know what she had in store for him. At least, if all went according to how she had it planned. The next few weeks would be busy with the play in less than two weeks, the Appleton Sales and Fest, and all the usual church activities she and her friends participated in. But somewhere in that time, she hoped to carry out a very special plan.

She had no idea where Jazzi was. She'd not been back to Amy's apartment since early this morning and wasn't here when Amy had come from the hospital. Amy had been hoping, with Jazzi's seeming break with Aaron—and the nice evening they'd all spent at Andy's art sale, that Jazzi had changed.

To her specifications? No, but to God's would be nice.

Pulling her favorite blanket up to her chin against the spring nighttime chill, Amy settled in her comfortable bed, ready for sleep. When her cell rang, she shook her head, hoping it was part of a dream, but the continual ringing finally pulled her eyes open. Stretching out a hand, she lifted her cell off the nightstand and stared at the screen.

Jazzi. As if her wondering about her sister had pulled a phone call from her.

She tapped the *answer* button. "Jazzi. Where are you?"

"Amy. Can you come? I think Aaron is going to kill someone."

What? Was this an attempt to scare Amy for a joke? Any minute now, would Amy hear her sister's chuckle?

"What do you mean, Jazzi? Are you serious?"

"Just come. I'm scared, Amy. Just come."

Throwing back the cover, Amy jumped from the bed, and reached for the first thing in sight to pull on. "Tell me where you are, Jazzi. I'll be there as soon as I can."

By the time Jazzi had whispered the address, Amy had grabbed her keys and was running down the stairs.

~*~

Amy fumbled with her cell as she sped down the dark road. If what Jazzi had said was true, her sister was in a peck of trouble, and Amy, by herself, couldn't handle a problem this big. She needed help, and as much as she'd love to have Toby at her side, Detective Eddie was the man to call.

When the man answered, Amy explained the situation. Detective Eddie assured her he'd meet her at the place, ordering her to not take matters into her own hands but wait till he arrived. Hopefully, she could get to Jazzi with no contact with Jazzi's ex-boyfriend. If not, all she could do was pray. She sure didn't want to tackle the man, maybe making the situation worse, but she wasn't about to let Jazzi get hurt if there was anything at all she could do.

The apartment where Jazzi had called from was dark. Amy parked her car, but saw no sign of Detective Eddie as of yet. But outside the apartment a man paced back and forth, shouting. She couldn't make out his words—and Amy assumed it was Aaron—but his tone was a barrel of drunken vitriol.

It was a two-story, apartment building, vintage with charming shutters and decorative eaves. Who lived here, and why was Jazzi here at all? An old,, old friend from school years? A new friend who wanted to party and hadn't known what trouble Jazzi carried around with her?

Ten minutes passed, and Detective Eddie still hadn't appeared. Amy bit her lip. Should she? Or not? Appleton's police chief would be furious if he caught her outside the car. But she wasn't going to confront Aaron. Just sneak around a bit and see if he had a gun. If there was a back door entrance, maybe she could get Jazzi out.

But if that was the case, why hadn't she already escaped?

Never mind. No time to dither.

Amy opened her door, and a hand shot out to stop it. She almost screamed. Almost. But the face that immediately peered at her had a finger at his lips.

Detective Eddie.

"What do you think you're doing?" The

whisper was accusatory and no-nonsense.

"No-nothing." Amy took a breath to still her stammering. "I wasn't going to approach Aaron. Just get close enough to see if he had a gun."

"I should send you home."

"Please don't. That's my sister in there."

"Very well. But you don't take a step without me saying so. He has a gun. Understand?"

He was going to let her go with him. Why? Usually cops ordered folk stay back from the problem. She didn't care.

"Let's go. And understand, Little Amy, there's only one reason you're going to be following in my footsteps tonight."

She opened her mouth to ask what that reason was, but he'd already turned away. Amy clamped her lips shut and tiptoed behind him as he advanced toward the still-shouting man.

Once in awhile he paused his loud demands to lift a bottle to his mouth, swipe at his lips, then stagger another few steps in his continual pacing, splitting the night with a mouthful of expletives.

When they stopped at the last available tree, Detective Eddie paused, motioned for her to stay put, and pulling his gun from his holster, advanced toward drunken Aaron.

Detective Eddie didn't point his pistol, only carried it at his side, and when he spoke it was quietly and calmly. "Okay, Aaron, don't you think it's time you go home and get some sleep?"

The other man whirled unsteadily and almost fell. "Who're you?"

"Just a man who doesn't want to see you get

hurt. Come on now."

"Hurt?" Aaron waved first his bottle then the gun. "She hurt me. Bad. Couldn't make her understand."

"Women have a tendency to do that at times." Detective Eddie took another few steps. "Come with me, and we can talk about it."

"No." Aaron swung back around, facing the apartment building again, his gun waving in the air. "Jazzi, you come down here right now. You have no right to hurt me like this. I mean it. Gonna have to take care of you."

The chief of police didn't wait any longer. He sprang at Aaron, and they both tumbled to the ground, but Aaron was on the bottom. Detective pulled his hands behind his back, cuffed him, and lifted him to his feet. Guiding him forward to his car, he paused and spoke to Amy. "Here's my reason for allowing you to follow me tonight."

It was all Amy could do to stand still and listen. But she knew better than to take off before Detective Eddie gave his nod of agreement.

"I got a phone call right after yours. The downstairs apartment resident—a highway patrol cop and a friend of mine—had already checked out the situation. I knew it was safe for you to follow as long as you did as I said." For the first time that evening, he smiled. "Now, get, Little Amy. Go for your sister, and you tell her, that I said she'd better hightail it back home with you. I want no more frightening events tonight. I have an early and long day tomorrow. I need my beauty sleep."

"Will do." Amy laughed. "Thank you,

Detective Eddie. You're the best chief in the world."

"You're right about that," he tossed back.

Amy didn't answer. She headed for the outside stairs that led to the upstairs apartment...and to her sister.

~*~

Toby made three phones calls the next morning. One to the hospital to find out about Ryle's condition. The answer was depressing. The doctors were worried that his friend hadn't awakened yet.

The second was to return a call from Detective Eddie. When he reached him, he'd filled him in on the previous night's activity with Aaron. Right now, Aaron was still sleeping off his drunken rage, but the chief planned on an intensive interview with the man later in the day. Hopefully, he'd get some answers.

The only thing that truly troubled Toby was Amy's involvement. Though Detective Eddie had assured him it hadn't been near as dangerous as it sounded, and that he'd made sure Amy was safe, it bothered him that she hadn't called.

His third call had been to Sharlene. As it turned out, she was delighted to hear from him.

"I was hoping you'd follow up on our dinner."

Really? After that kiss with Gordon?

"Would you like to go to dinner again? Or lunch, if you prefer?"

"Dinner sounds great. Apple Blossoms again?"

"Sure. I'll pick you up at seven."

"No, don't bother. I'll meet you there."

Rats. He'd hoped to make it easy on himself and find out in one swoop where she was staying and if she was connected to the trespassing.

But there was more than one way to skin a cat, as many West Virginians were prone to say. And he knew just how to go about it.

Chapter Fifteen

If there was one thing Amy didn't want to do, it was go out with Gordon Rickward. A fickle man—or woman—was low on her list of desirable traits. But for their cause, she'd do it. When he suggested Apple Blossoms, she heartily agreed. Suited her plans perfectly. And Toby's.

She and Toby had decided that if possible, to guide their dates' decision on the place, as Apple Blossoms. They'd make sure Manny, the maître d, knew their plans and chose secluded seating arrangements close together.

Amy couldn't care less what she wore on a date with Gordon. She wasn't trying to impress him, but Apple Blossoms was too high class to not do so.

And then there was Toby.

Toby.

He'd been really upset at her for tagging along with Detective Eddie last night. He'd get over it. Still, he seldom showed that much tense emotion around her, so what did that say about his feelings? She kind of liked him worried about her. He had to like her a lot. At least, she hoped so.

It was time to get ready for Tuesday night's rehearsal. Only two more weeks till opening night.

First things first. She'd make a short stop at the hospital to check on Ryle and talk to him a bit even though he was still unconscious. The doctors had assured her that the CAT scans showed no danger signs in his brain, and after he rested, he should revive and be his old self.

It wouldn't hurt to make sure he understood—even if he didn't respond—that she was expecting him to recover. He needed to be at the play opening on the first day of Appleton's Sales and Fest, and she wasn't about to be disappointed in that.

~*~

As it turned out, Amy was fifteen minutes late. She exited her car and flew into the theater, shedding her light jacket as she ran.

Rehearsal hadn't started yet, so she called out to one of the ladies who assisted with the costumes, "Where's Toby?"

"Last time I saw him he was on his phone." The woman hurried off, carrying a bundle of clothes.

"Toby?" She called out as she slipped behind the curtain. "Why haven't you start—?"

Toby stood with his back to her, his fists clenched into knots as he slowly turned toward her.

Her words trailed off as she caught a glimpse of his face. "What's wrong?"

"We're done."

A dagger pierced her heart. Was he talking about their relationship—casual that it was? "What do you mean, done?"

"Haven't you heard? Krissy and Jason ran off."

"No."

"It's true."

Amy sank into a nearby chair. "I can't believe that. After all the work we've put in at church trying to steer them right..." Her voice trailed off as a thought struck her.

Toby spoke before she could put it into words. "We now have no leading lady and man."

Her heart sank at his discouragement. He always put so much of himself into each play, pushing his actors to achieve more than they thought they could. And succeeded too. There had never been one play that the town hadn't given them a standing ovation.

Until now.

"What are we going to do?"

"What else to do but cancel?"

"What you're going to do is go on with the play."

Amy turned at the same time as Toby to gape at the man walking slowly toward them, a huge grin on his face.

Ryle Sadler had just returned to life.

~*~

"Ryle. What are you doing out of bed?" Amy hurried across the floor and slipped an arm around him.

Toby shoved a chair at him. "Sit before you fall."

Laughing, Ryle sat. "I'm okay. Weak, but okay."

"You shouldn't be out of bed. I can't believe they released you," Amy scolded.

"They didn't. I didn't tell them I was leaving. Just did."

"But why? You could have a setback."

"I'm not going to have a setback. Except for being weak from no food for four days, I feel great. As if I just woke up from a much-needed nap."

When Toby could get a word in edgewise, he asked, "What did you mean, 'you're going to go on with the play'? How can we? We just lost our two main actors. There's no time to recruit others even if there were any."

"Nonsense. We have two perfect ones already here in the play. I bet they even know most, if not all the lines. They'll be a slam dunk with the audience."

He was still grinning like the Cheshire cat.

"Who on earth are you talking about?"

"Why..." Ryle dragged out his response. "...who else? You and Amy."

~*~

Toby ended up canceling rehearsal that night. He was far too discouraged—combined with Ryle's sudden appearance and suggestion—to even think straight, alone consider the outrageous idea.

Toby pulled his car into the drive of Undiscovered Treasures and stared at his business. He was too restless to go to sleep. What he needed was a short, brisk run. He wasn't exactly dressed in the most comfortable clothes—except for his shoes—but they'd do.

Just maybe Detective Eddie would still be at the police station. Toby could swing by and see if he'd gotten Aaron to talk.

Toby locked his car door, and headed out in a fast walk, breathing deeply of the night air. How he loved this state, this town, and the people. He couldn't imagine living anywhere else.

Yeah, are you planning on living here all your life by your lonesome?

The words popped into his mind, and he

wanted to groan. He hadn't wanted to do any introspective examination on this walk. Definitely not tonight. And preferably not about this subject.

But the thought would not leave him.

He wanted to argue with himself. "I have my sister."

You had Caro. She now has Andy.

Why did that sound so reasonable?

"I like having my own apartment. I like being on my own."

Ha. How long will that last? Growing old and lonely is no fun, let me tell you that.

"I'd prefer not to hear that depressing bit of news."

Great. Now he was talking to his inner self. Out loud, at that. Toby picked up his pace, pushing himself to run faster.

As he approached the pond, he slowed, catching his breath, and paused beside the tallest pine tree in town. He allowed his eyes to close, hoping he could erase the distressing thoughts from moments ago.

It was then he heard the low voices.

Toby straightened. Where were they coming from?

He sneaked a quick look around the area, but saw nothing except the normal nature scene. The murmurs hadn't stopped.

He edged around the tree and tried to focus on the voices and realized they were coming from about twenty feet away. It was dark. The kind of dark books wrote about in scary scenes. If he hadn't known this path like the back of his hand, he might have stumbled or taken a careless tumble into the pond.

But he did know it, and that wasn't the

reason he hadn't seen the persons talking.

The two voices were on the other side of that big oak fifteen or so feet from him, just off the path.

Time to move closer. He risked being heard, true. But he couldn't risk not hearing what those two people were doing out here this time of the night. Definitely not what he was doing. Introspective thinking while running to clear his mind. Ha.

Stalking it was then, and Toby wasted no time in moving. He was a fast runner, so if he had to make a getaway, he might be able to do it successfully. Hopefully, he wouldn't have to run for his life. And he almost chuckled at the thought, but didn't.

"I'm done covering for you. The old man's done with you. You can't even complete one task without getting into trouble—"

"That was nothing. I'm close. I know it. You have to talk with him. Make him understand."

"Make him understand what? That you're a loser?"

Feet shuffled. One of them coughed.

These two weren't children or teenagers. More like men in their late twenties or thirties, the one confident and scornful.

"He likes me the best."

That voice was definitely sulky, petulant as if used to being mocked.

"I'm finished...

"You're finished?" The second voice yelled. "He's done—with you."

Sounded as if those two were done all right. Done talking. He must have just come at the end of their conversation. Toby took a step backward, and a branch snapped.

"What was that?"

"An animal. I've got to run. You've got this week, then I wash my hands. I've got more important things to do. And I can't wait till I get out of this hillbilly state."

There was movement, then the confident man warned, "Don't mess up."

Toby stepped behind a large bush and held his breath as first one, then the other man passed him by, not giving him so much as a glance.

But then it *was* dark.

Toby's fortunate night.

~*~

"What are you doing out here, Toby? Don't you know it's dangerous to be out this time of the night?"

The low voice, with the thread of amusement in it, came from his right and startled him for a moment. Just until he realized who it was speaking to him.

Detective Eddie.

"I could ask you the same question, but I guess I shouldn't since you're the police around here. Anyhow, I'm not afraid of the dark. It would be the people that inhabit it that I would be wary of."

"You're right about that. I don't suppose you got a glimpse of those two."

"Nope. You?"

"Afraid not. Only now came upon you."

"You're not following me, are you?" Toby couldn't keep the suspicion from his voice.

"Maybe a tad bit. Just enough to ease a certain female mind."

"Amy?" Now she was having him followed?

"I didn't say who." The detective chuckled.

"Right. You don't have to." He wouldn't have kept the sarcasm from his voice if he'd wanted to. Amy had no right...Whoa. She was a friend. A concerned friend. The one he'd run to when he'd wanted to talk about all the break-ins.

"Could be your sister."

"I suppose you're right." Toby agreed, but he knew. It wasn't Caro.

"Anything interesting?"

"Sounded like two friends arguing. Maybe a business deal? One of them messed up, and the other was disgusted over the fact."

"Hmm."

Toby began walking, and the police chief kept up.

"Aaron say anything when you put him in jail?"

"Are you kidding? He could hardly stay awake long enough to talk. I practically had to carry him inside."

"Crazy guy. Not sure I care much for him. Sounds like a loser."

You're a loser.

The words of the man just off the path echoed in Toby's mind. Why had he spoken the same ones? Two losers in town...

"He's out now though."

Detective Eddie was speaking again, but Toby halted his fast walk to stare at the man.

They'd left the woods and reentered the town.

"How could he have done that?"

"The man who got him out went to the county judge and posted bail."

"This time of the night?" Really? "Why didn't

you let me know?"

"It's wasn't tonight. Early this afternoon, and I wanted to call you but had an important summons to meet with Lin—an undercover agent. Couldn't back out of that." The man beside him shrugged. "Some strings were pulled. I think this guy—Rickward?—knew some people who knew some people, and worked out some kind of arrangement."

"Is that legal?"

A cock of the head and raised brow was all the answer Toby got.

"I'll do some checking in the morning, which will be here before I get my beauty sleep, if you don't head home soon."

"Heading that way now. You don't need to babysit me all the way, do you?"

"As long as you *go* there." Detective Eddie gave him a wave and a nod, then called back over his shoulder. "Gotta keep my promise, you know."

Toby watched him go and wanted to be irritated at the man, but he wasn't. If Toby and Amy's places had been reversed, he would have appreciated that Detective Eddie was keeping his promises.

He unlocked his front door and turned to stare down the street. The man was gone, but Toby's mind was more active than ever.

Aaron and Rickward?

~*~

This was the hardest thing Toby had ever done. From the time he'd wakened this morning, instead of pondering over the Rickward and Aaron situation from last night, this was filling his mind. Demanding an answer.

He knew he couldn't put off deciding.

He stood by the front desk of his business and stared down at his cell lying on the counter top.

Why was it so hard? There were only two answers. Yes. Or no.

But he'd never done this—well, except for school plays, and that had been a few years ago.

So what was it to be? Should he and Amy take the lead parts in Caro's newest play?

The door-bell jingled, and Amy entered, carrying a bunch of papers that looked suspiciously like the play script.

"I've been carrying this thing around all day, trying to decide whether I would be the dumbest person in the world to attempt this, or the latest, greatest actor. Somehow, I seriously doubted the last option."

"I know." Toby clenched his teeth to keep back the groan. "I tried to ignore it yesterday, but today—knowing we have rehearsal tonight if we go on with the play—I can't get this out of my mind. I've been distracted all day."

"Have you talked with Ryle?"

"No. I assumed he was resting up."

"He's planning on being at rehearsal tonight. I told him I wasn't sure if you were canceling or not, but he laughed and said you wouldn't cancel."

"Really? What has happened to him since that crack on the head?"

"Who knows? But he sure is more talkative and confident. Or so he seems."

"Maybe it was there all the time, but he wouldn't let it show."

"I always said, remember, there was a mystery about him."

"And we still don't know what it is and probably never will."

"What are we going to do?"

"About this?" Toby pointed at the script now lying on the counter top.

"Yeah."

Toby studied the papers. Would it be so hard? He knew the thing from cover to cover, had memorized all the lines easily enough seeing he'd been studying it for a half year now. Ever since Caro had laid it down in front of him months ago.

But to show the emotion needed in front of all the town? With Amy as his co-actor?

He did groan then. "It's either do it or disappoint the town's people. They're expecting it the first night of the fest."

"I know."

He glanced down one more time at the script, then raised his gaze to meet Amy's.

"We have no choice. We've got to try."

Amy stretched out a hand and gripped his. "We'd better do a whole lot of praying. God help us."

~*~

As far as Toby was concerned, rehearsal that night was a mess. Disheartened, the cast members' performance was lackadaisical, Ryle wasn't there to fill in as director, and Toby and Amy were as awkward as two twelve-year-olds in grade school. The other actors were filing out of the theater, silent and morose—and no wonder with the discouraging evening.

Amy was on the other side of the stage, ignoring him and, he figured, as uncertain about the success of this play as he was.

The outer door opened, and Detective Eddie filed in. Behind him came Ryle Sadler, both men as sober as the proverbial judge.

Toby watched them coming, hoping the news wasn't as dismal as the rest of the evening had been.

"News, Toby." Detective Eddie and Ryle walked up the stairs.

"What now?"

Ryle took a deep breath. "I've remembered something else."

"I take it, it pertains to what's been happening."

"Nothing major—maybe, but it could be important."

"Then give."

"I remember you asked me to keep an eye on that old man Cowell, so I did. Four hours' worth." Ryle gave Toby a wry grin. "Not much happened at first."

"Doesn't sound hopeful."

"No, not until later. I did notice that when you began your bidding, he seemed to perk up with interest, then immediately turned his attention to something or someone else."

"How does this help?"

"It doesn't. But when I slipped out for just a few seconds, I lost him. I searched everywhere and thought he'd left. Just happened to see him with those two men you hired to transport what you bought. He only spent seconds with them—almost like a casual greeting in passing type of thing—but what surprised me was the look in his eyes."

"What kind of look?"

"The kind that says 'you know what to do' or 'get this done'."

"Are you sure?"

"I've been around a bit. Do a fair job of reading expressions."

"Seems serious to me, if he had anything to do with stealing Toby's van and furniture and injuring you." Detective Eddie smoothed his mustache.

"I can't see any reason why that man would be interested in my van or furniture. What he wanted was already in my shop and sold. He was angry over that."

"Could be a fluke in conversation," Detective Eddie offered, but the doubt in his voice belied the statement. "He might have been talking about a job totally different than yours, Toby. Even one he hired them to do at that auction. Could have feared they'd forget or put yours ahead of his."

"Makes sense."

"Well, I stand by my assessment of the situation." Ryle laughed.

"You do that, Ryle." Detective slapped him on the shoulder. "Now for my news, and a bit more obvious than Ryle's."

"Okay, give." Was anything going to go good for a change?

"My contact found Aaron's last name."

"And?"

"Evanston."

Disappointment rushed through Toby. How did Detective Eddie think that helped?

"But the best part..."

There was more?

"...his mother's maiden name was Cowell."

"That means—"

"Right. Unless it's a one in a million coincidence, Aaron and your Mr. Cowell are related."

"Do you know the relationship? Was Aaron's mother old man Cowell's daughter?"

"Yes. Seems there was a split between the two when she ran off to marry a man Cowell didn't approve of."

"Seems the plot thickens." Toby joked.

"Did Mr. Cowell make up with his daughter or the grandson?" Amy's question went straight to the heart of the discussion.

"From what I heard, the daughter and her husband died when Aaron was still young. Barnabas Cowell took the boy in and raised him as his son."

"Wow. Do you suppose they're in this together?"

"Meaning what, Little Amy?" Detective Eddie's mouth twitched upward.

"Meaning, did they conspire to break into Toby's business? And mine?"

"There's not much, if any, proof either did. Some vague statements. Toby's sighting of a man in an empty building." Detective Eddie shook his head. "We can't jump to conclusions."

"Then how do we go about getting concrete evidence?"

Whoever had caused the mischief, the break-ins, Toby knew he needed to put it behind him. He could just forget the whole thing. After all, there hadn't been any more for a couple weeks now. But there was the stolen van and Ryle's attack. That definitely said someone was still interested in his business or something to do with him.

"I am going to talk to both of them. Not sure if I'll get answers, but, hopefully, it will clear up a few things." Detective Eddie's hand went to his mustache again.

"At least it might eliminate the two of them."

"We'll see."

They were back to square one if these two were not involved. But Toby wasn't quitting. He should leave the detecting to the town's chief of police. He should never have talked about this mess with Amy and involved her. He should never have asked Ryle to keep an eye on Cowell.

A lot of should-never-haves.

But an idea was tickling his mind. He couldn't quite grasp it, but he would.

Chapter Sixteen

Toby double-checked the suit he wore in the mirror. He'd elected to copy Andy's style—in as much as he could with the off-the-rack suit selection from the local shop here in town versus Andy's smart, Paris one-of-a-kind suit—but, if he did say so himself, he thought he didn't appear too shabby.

He'd taken time to get a haircut, he was nice and tan—even if it was still spring—and he'd even sprung for a small bouquet of orchids—unlike the lilacs Amy adored—for Sharlene, hoping it would soften her up a bit when he began asking questions. If, he did.

Depended on her mood, he knew, and probably whether she was involved in anything shady. If so, he knew she'd turn on that million-dollar-smile and bypass any answer he hoped to get from her.

Still, it was worth a shot.

Manny, at Apple Blossoms, had agreed to make sure both he and Sharlene and Amy and that Rickward man had secluded seats. Not too obvious, of course, but enough so he and Amy could keep track of each other.

Toby was just locking the front door, preparing to leave, when his cell rang, and he stared down at the name. Sharlene. Had something happened? Was she going to be late? Maybe she wanted him to pick her up after all.

He'd never know unless he answered. "Hello, Sharlene."

"Oh, Toby. I'm so sorry, but I can't make it."

She sounded distressed although he could tell she was struggling to keep calm.

"Is something wrong? Are you okay?"

"I'm...fine. Just some things have come up with my client, and I have to take care of them. He won't let me postpone."

"Then don't worry a thing about it. Would you want to grab a late coffee at The Coffee House?"

"I wish I could, but I can't."

Was that a bit of impatience in her voice?

"Maybe someday soon." She hung up then.

Toby lowered his phone and stared down at it. Someday soon? What did that mean? Or was it a polite way of getting rid of him?

Amy.

She'd be expecting him to show up, and he wouldn't be there. Pressing the button to speed dial her number, he listened as it rang five times, then her recording came on, and Toby left a message. Either she'd left her phone at home or couldn't answer right now. Either way, she'd get it eventually and know why he hadn't shown.

Should he call Manny and have him pass on a message, just in case?

Pressing a different number, the Apple Blossom number rang, and it seconds, the desk receptionist answered. When he asked to speak to Manny, she put him on hold, but in seconds, he answered.

"Apple Blossoms maître'd, Manny here."

"Manny. It's Toby Gibson. Something's come up and I can't make that reservation tonight.

Can you pass on a quiet message to Amy and let her know she's on her own?"

With the assurance from Manny that he would, Toby hung up.

Unlocking his door, he headed back upstairs to change once again into more comfortable clothes when his cell rang again.

"Toby here."

"Getting ready to question Mr. Cowell and his grandson. Wanna listen in?"

It was Detective Eddie, and Toby didn't have to think about it. He certainly did want to listen in.

~*~

Amy didn't want to dress up too formally for her dinner with Gordon. Apple Blossoms was an upscale restaurant, true, but she wasn't worried about being underdressed. Starli would understand her reasoning. It was Gordon she was nervous about.

He'd given definite indications he was interested in her, yet days later she saw him kissing that friend of Toby's. And that kiss wasn't a brother giving his sister a *welcome home* peck on the cheek. No, the kiss between those two had been passionate and real.

What did that say about the man? Fickle? Dense? Insincere? Whatever he was, she wanted no part in it.

She finally settled on a swingy, flowered skirt and plain silk blouse. Looping a matching scarf around her neck, Amy frowned at her image. She looked like a business woman instead of a woman out for dinner with a friend. But since she wasn't at all sure Gordon and her relationship could be classified as friendship, she supposed she'd do.

Now if she was going out with Toby...

Amy snapped the window closed on the thought trying to derail her plans for tonight.

When the doorbell rang, Amy gave it five seconds before opening the door.

Gordon was quite the dashing gentleman, and his manner was polite, even though he seemed distracted. Not a good sign.

Or was it?

The drive was a short one, and after Manny had seated them at their table, Amy broached a couple different, inane topics, hoping to capture his attention. When that didn't work, she took matters head-on in her hands.

"Gordon, are you all right? Would you rather skip dinner?"

"What?" Gordon's gaze refocused on Amy. "I'm sorry. I'm expecting an important phone call. That's certainly no reason to ignore you. What were you saying?"

"I was saying, our town fest starts Tuesday next week. Will you be staying long enough to take it in?"

"I'm not sure. Depends."

That was telling her nothing. Why did he hedge so much on giving her a direct answer?

"Business calling you back to the big city, is it?" She grinned to take the edge off her nosiness—if that could be done.

"That too."

"I'm sure you'd enjoy the fest. It's a family time, besides giving our shops a lot of business. We have crafters selling at booths, shops giving heavy discounts, the children and teens put on skits and their parents manage the contests. I think my friend Caro is even giving away a treasure chest this year."

When Gordon's gaze focused on her this time, it was with a sharpness that indicated intense interest. "That sounds like fun. What's in this chest?"

Amy shrugged. "Who knows but Caro? She's whimsical. It could be a wide variety of items from unique salt and pepper shakers to jewels. Whatever's in the chest will make some child happy if he or she finds it."

"So it's for children only?"

"Not at all. Grownups will enjoy searching for it."

"I see. So no guarantees?"

"None." She gave him a sly glance. "But I wouldn't miss it. Who knows? I'm anxious to search too."

"Would you go as my partner if I stay?" He cocked his head, amusement in his eyes.

"Why not?" She didn't want to, but if it kept him here a little longer, she'd do it. Just until she found what she wanted to know.

"Then I'll count on it." Gordon stared at her, his dark eyes unblinking, a smile on his lips. "Did you know there's a rumor around town that someone's been breaking into your business?"

"Once. True."

The man opposite her said nothing more about the break-ins, and as much as Amy hinted, and even a couple times asked pointed questions pertaining to his business and family, she came up with no information that was helpful.

When they at last left their table, Gordon took her arm and led her outside, his smile just as bright as when he'd picked her up earlier and his comments as noncommittal as ever.

Chapter Seventeen

"**I** wish we could ask Amy to listen in, but she's busy tonight." Toby was at the chief of police's office, waiting on Detective Eddie to question Barnabas Cowell and his grandson, Aaron.

"I thought about it, but didn't want to pull her into it any more than was necessary. She doesn't need to hear the dirty details of these men's doings."

Toby wasn't at all sure Amy would agree with Detective Eddie's assessment of her. She might be little but she had the courage of a lion when facing obstacles.

"How is she doing? I heard she's been hanging around that suave Rickward fellow. Word has it, they had no eyes for anyone but each other. She needs to be careful."

"People like to gossip, even in our small community." Toby wanted to scowl but stopped himself before giving away his feelings. She was *not* interested in that cad. She'd said so herself.

Detective Eddie's only staff member—other than the dispatcher—stuck his head in the room. "Cowell and his grandson are here, Chief."

"Put them in Interrogation Room One, Officer."

"Yes, Sir."

It didn't matter how many times Detective Eddie talked with suspects, didn't matter that he had only *one* room to question people, he always referred to the room the same as if he had several *interrogation* rooms. It'd been pointed out to him more than one time, but he acknowledged the statement no more than he would have a pesky fly.

The man was priceless. Ever since the previous Chief had retired, Eddie, who'd been the first chief's only detective, had filled the empty position. He did such a great job no one had bothered hiring a new chief. Now, residents of Appleton chose—as their mood changed—chief or Detective Eddie as the man's title. No one but outsiders thought a thing about it. *Those* were Eddie's jobs, and he filled them perfectly. Thank you very much.

Now, Toby stared through the window into the next room. No matter what the movies portrayed, Appleton's only window where officers and others could watch the proceedings, was small and old, making the process of observation anything but pleasant. But the sound was great, and Toby had no trouble listening to the conversation in the other room.

"Thanks for coming in, Mr. Cowell," Detective Eddie began.

The chief's pleasant tone didn't deceive Toby. The Appleton chief was well-known for his technique of questioning. More than one criminal had found himself confessing to a misdeed and not even realizing it.

"Why are we here?" Mr. Cowell snapped, not in the least intimidated by Detective Eddie.

"I need to clear up a few matters besides seeing if you can answer a few questions I have."

"I see no reason why you'd think I can help."

"Perhaps not."

Toby wanted to cringe at Detective Eddie's deceptively calm tone.

"Is it true you've been involved in several scandals?" The chief didn't stop there. "Is it true several members in your family have been suspected of crimes?"

"And never convicted." Mr. Cowell roared his answer.

Toby took particular note of Aaron reaching across the space and gently laying a hand on the older man's. But the old man wasn't having any gentle reminders to keep his cool.

He half rose in his seat. "Is that what you brought us down here for?"

Detective Eddie didn't immediately answer the question. When he did, he changed the subject.

"What drew you to a small town like Appleton?"

This time it did take Cowell by surprise as if walloped on the side of the head by a thick, heavy-handed person. The lines in his face deepened, but his gaze didn't waver as he studied the small-town cop. "Is that a crime here?"

"Not at all. Just filling in some blanks."

The calm reply seemed to soothe the older man's irritation, and he answered petulantly. "I wanted to retire somewhere quiet and where I could be left alone to pursue my special interests. I was tired of big city life."

"I see." Detective Eddie sat back in his seat as if having a friendly chat with a buddy. "Are you sure you didn't want to take your grandson away from—let's say, less than desirable companions? Are you sure you weren't trying to rescue him from himself?"

"What? That's stupid." Mr. Cowell gave the chief his best sniff of disdain.

"Is it? Let's try this: what are your special interests? Is this a hobby?"

Ask him if it's antiques! Toby shouted at the detective in his mind.

Obviously, the chief of police wasn't ready to hear the other man's answers. "Art collector? Jewels? Stamps? *Antiques*?"

If someone hadn't been watching they'd never have seen the imperceptible quiver in Cowell's jaw. But Toby did, and he was sure it hadn't escaped Detective Eddie's attention.

"Does it matter? How do my interests help you? How does it fill in blanks?"

But Detective Eddie wasn't in any mood to answer questions, just spin them out at breakneck speed. He switched targets. "Aaron Evanston—it is Evanston, isn't it? You didn't take your grandfather's name, by any chance, did you?"

"No. Why ask me? You think you know everything."

"Not quite, but close."

No one could best Detective Eddie in sarcasm.

"And what about these charges, Aaron?" Detective Eddie laid out a sheet of paper. "Breaking and entering. Theft. Assault."

"Don't answer that, Aaron." Cowell snapped the order. "Do we need an attorney?"

"I'm just asking questions. Do you think you need one?"

The chief leaned forward, propping his

elbows on the table. "Did you break into Undiscovered Treasures in March? What were you looking for, Aaron? We know you have a history of breaking and entering, that your reputation is a quick pick-up of what you're after and leaving immediately."

"No. I've quit all that. I didn't do it."

"What were you after, Aaron? Didn't find it, did you?"

The young man was shaking his head, but Detective Eddie wasn't done talking.

"Did you also break into Amy Sanderson's flower shop? Why would you think the *it* you were looking for, would be there? Hmmm. In a flower shop? Who would hide something in a flower shop?"

Aaron refused to answer, but Detective surged on. "How well do you know Gordon Rickward?"

"I don't."

"Nonsense. He's the one who posted bail for you."

When Aaron shot a quick glance at his grandfather, Detective Eddie switched targets. "Mr. Cowell, how do you know this Rickward fellow?"

"That's enough. We're done." Cowell shoved back his chair. "Sounds like you have nothing and are on a fishing trip. If you're not arresting either of us, we're leaving."

"Oh, I'm not done yet, but you're free to go for now. Don't leave town, Cowell, or you either, Evanston. We'll have more questions."

Cowell sneered and dragged his grandson from the room.

Detective Eddie gathered up his folder and

followed the two out of the interrogation room. When he stepped into the adjoining observation room where Toby stood, and his officer sat, recording the session, Detective Eddie was whistling.

Now, what did the detective have to whistle about? Sounded like a total bust to Toby.

~*~

Amy opened her eyes, but everything was blurry. She shook her head, and tried to roll over but couldn't. She wiggled, her mind clearing, and realized what was wrong.

She was tied up and lying on a bed.

It was light in the room, so she'd been here—wherever that was—all night.

Relaxing her muscles, she tried to think how she came to be in such a condition. She remembered having dinner with Gordon. He'd been the perfect gentleman, walking her to her door. She hadn't had to worry about fending him off with unwelcome advances. He'd gripped her hand and said a soft good-bye before turning to leave.

She'd unlocked her door, stepped inside and reached for the light switch. That's when it'd happened. Someone had been waiting inside for her.

Why?

If only she'd screamed or struggled or something.

But she hadn't been able to. She remembered a firm grip and...a cloth. The person had chloroformed her. Or had it been two people?

Her gaze swept around the room. Looked pretty ordinary to her. Almost...sterile, but not quite. There was nothing close at hand to help break her bonds. She wiggled again, trying to get an idea of how tightly she was bound.

Too tight.

Off in the distance, she heard footsteps that gradually drew closer. Someone was coming. Should she feign sleep or stay wide awake and demand answers?

And who on earth was her captor?

Chapter Eighteen

Once Barnabas Cowell and Aaron left the police station, Toby sat down beside Detective Eddie's desk.

"What now? You sounded awfully chipper after they took off."

"Best way to set them on edge—if they're guilty, and sometimes it works on those with not a guilty bone in their bodies." Detective Eddie shuffled papers.

"So what do you think? Did you learn anything from them? What do we do now?"

"*You* do nothing. This is out of your hands, Toby Gibson. Don't make me put you in a cell for safety's sake."

"Good grief, detective. I'm not a kid."

"That you're not."

"Well, at least tell me what *you're* going to do now?"

For the first time, Detective Eddie looked at Toby. "Dig deeper, Toby. Dig deeper."

"So you do think they're guilty, don't you?"

"Of something, yes."

"Of what?"

"There's a connection between Rickward and Aaron, and I suspect Mr. Cowell too. Have no idea what. Yet."

"How are you going to find out?"

"First things first. I'll have my officer spend a few nights watching them."

"He can't do that continuously."

"Figured I'd give you a call about then." There went his hand to his mustache.

"But you just said to stay away—"

"Just until—unless—I need you."

Toby sat back. "I see."

"Then I'll have the dispatcher do some serious searching for some ideas those two gave me. He never has enough to do anyway."

Better ignore that last comment. "What kind of ideas?"

"Specifically? Cowell's interests. Why Aaron ended up with his grandfather. Why the young man was in so much trouble. Ideas like those. Figure we find the answers to those questions and any others that pop up, and we'll be able to pinpoint who's guilty."

"You really think so?"

"Sure. Now you get on home. I've got work to do."

And with that Detective Eddie proceeded to ignore Toby.

Toby chuckled to himself. He didn't care what Detective Eddie said. He was going to do his own research. He wasn't known as a computer whiz for no reason.

~*~

Early the next morning, after his daily run, Toby was at his computer downstairs in Undiscovered Treasures shop. He'd tried to call Amy before his run, but there had been no answer. No doubt she was catching a few hours extra sleep after the date last night. He just hoped it hadn't been too late of a date. That wouldn't bode well for their relationship.

His heart insisted: *why should you care?* But he ignored the nosy organ. He didn't have time to answer crazy questions.

He had a busy day lined up, with finishing up the list of items that would go on sale during the Appleton Fest, rehearsal tonight—and hopefully, it would go better than the other night, or they might as well wash their hands of the whole thing—and doing the research on the idea that had emerged from his mind. He had one hour before the shop opened...

Now to see what he could discover.

His fingers tapped rapidly as he moved from one article to the next, searching and hoping he'd find what he wanted. When he found nothing on his first specific search, he switched gears and subjects.

And then he paused and re-read what he'd just scanned through.

Bingo!

Chapter Nineteen

The footsteps grew louder...and then paused. A key scratched against the lock, there was a click, and the door opened. A figure stood in the doorway, a sad smile—anything but reassuring—on the face of the person gazing at Amy.

Walking toward her, the person said, "I want to release you, but you've got to be good. Will you? I want to talk with you. Sorry it had to be this way, but you and Toby Gibson have been in the way from the beginning." The person released her hands and pulled down the gag from her mouth.

Amy's first instinct was to lash out, but caution won out. It was too soon. This person—this one she had trusted and liked—what had caused the sudden departure from civility?

"Why are you doing this? If you tell me what you want, I can help."

"Can you? I think the question is: will you?"

"Of course, I will if I can."

The other person stared at her with a dark-eyed gaze. "Where is it?"

"Where is *what*?"

"Why did I know you'd say that? If I knew the answer to that, I would have already taken it. You're no help. Let's see if a few more minutes tied up will loosen your tongue a little more."

"Why on earth do you think I know what you're looking for? I have no idea."

"You need a bathroom break?"

When Amy nodded, the person led her to the small room and partially closed the door. Once Amy had finished, the person led her to the bed but made no more comments, only re-tied Amy's hands and made sure the gag was securely around her mouth. Without another glance, the person left, locking the door.

~*~

"Amy, I need to talk with you ASAP. Call me." Toby hung up. This was the third time he'd tried to reach her. Where could she be? Out shopping with Jazzi?

No. She seldom took long breaks from her regular work hours. It was almost time for closing here at his own business. Maybe he'd better stop by Bloomin' Life and see what was going on.

Amy had put herself into the few practices they had to get ready for opening night, but Toby could tell she felt awkward. That was nothing compared to his own uncomfortableness. He was very much afraid, for the first time ever, this summer's play was destined to be a disaster. He should have listened to his instincts and never asked Krissy and Jason to perform as co-leading actors.

Too late for regrets now.

Locking the door, Toby hurried around the vacant building and entered Bloomin' Life. One of Amy's temporary employees manned the front desk, unenthusiastically. "Hi. Is Amy around?"

"No. Ryle's in charge." She shrugged. "I supposed Amy took the day off. Haven't seen her."

That was strange. She seldom did that and, lately, let him know when it happened. "Ryle in the back?"

The woman didn't bother looking up but nodded, and Toby headed to the greenhouse where Ryle usually spent his time when he filled in for one of Amy's employees.

He was replenishing her supply of mulch, stacking the bags neatly against the back wall.

"Hey, Ryle. Have you seen Amy today?"

"No." Ryle stopped his work and wiped at his forehead. "When one of the employees called me, I tried to get ahold of her, but she didn't answer her phone. Figured I'd better show up, just keep everything in line till she returned."

"Did you try talking with Jazzi?"

"Tried, but she didn't answer her phone either. I assumed they'd gone into Charleston shopping."

"Doesn't sound like Amy. She never deserts her responsibilities."

"I thought so too, but didn't want to sound an alarm over nothing." Ryle turned away and lifted yet another bag from the cart.

Toby eyed the man. His comment sounded off. Where was all the concern for their friend? "Okay. I'll check around. See you tonight?"

"Sure thing."

Again, Toby eyed the man who still had his back to him. Was he avoiding any more conversation with him for a reason?

Walking out of Bloomin' Life, Toby pulled out his cell, tried Amy again, and when there was no answer, punched in Detective Eddie's number. The man answered in his usual laid-back manner.

"Just thought I should alert you. Amy's not answering her phone."

"Sick?"

"Amy? No. I don't think so. I think she would have told someone, and no one that I can find, has heard anything from her. That's not like her. Ryle showed up at her shop to oversee everything, but he's not heard from her either. Just took the initiative to do so."

"Hmm. I can swing by her apartment."

"I have a key. We exchanged one day, just in case either of us had an emergency."

Silence. Than another, "Hmm."

"I'll meet you there in fifteen minutes."

Thirteen minutes later, Toby pulled into Amy's driveway at her parents' home. His heart sank as he saw her bright blue car sitting in the driveway.

Chapter Twenty

Toby debated for all of two seconds about waiting for Detective Eddie to arrive. He couldn't be more than a couple minutes behind him, but Toby was in no mood to wait. What if Amy was hurt? Every minute might mean life or death.

He could be letting his imagination run wild, but he didn't think so. Jiggling the key in the lock to her apartment till it finally clicked, Toby opened the door, and the silence was as heavy as a cloud-laden sky.

But what sent his heart into a tail spin for the second time in less than an hour was the blue and black-flower-laden tote bag lying on the floor just inside the entry way.

She never dumped her possessions around. Neat and tidy, everything she owned had a place. On the floor wasn't one of those.

"Amy?" His call to her was cautious, but he wasted no time moving further into the apartment. But two minutes later, he knew Amy was not in the apartment. There was no signs of disturbance—except for the tote lying on the entry way floor.

"Toby, you in there?"

It was Detective Eddie.

"Yeah." Toby hurried to the front of the apartment. "She's not here."

"You should have waited on me."

He wasn't about to argue with Detective

Eddie. He wouldn't win the debate. "This is the only thing I found out of place."

Detective Eddie squatted and studied the bag. "Nothing else disturbed?"

"Nothing. She always keeps her place spotless. I'm afraid—"

"Let's not jump to conclusions. Her sister might have called and needed her."

"Or someone kidnapped her." The tote on the floor spelled out nothing but trouble to Toby. Regardless of Detective Eddie's cautionary tone.

The detective pondered the bag again then stood. "Makes no sense. I'll have dispatch put out a bulletin on her, but it's not been twenty-four hours. Could be nothing."

"I can't take that chance."

Detective Eddie switched his stare to Toby. "I'm afraid you're right."

~*~

"I've got to meet someone tonight. After that I may have some interesting information that will help us," Toby said as he and Detective Eddie headed to their respective vehicles.

"We're keeping an eye on Cowell and his grandson. So far, nothing."

Toby's phone rang. Caro. "Hey, Sis—"

"I just heard that Amy's missing. Do you know anything about this?"

"I've been trying to find out. You haven't heard anything else?"

"No. Wait. I did see her last night at Apple Blossoms."

"By herself?"

"No. She was with some handsome guy."

Gordon Rickward?

"Were you there? Did you see them?" Toby

motioned to Detective Eddie.

"Andy and I were having dinner with Starli and Joel. They sat across the restaurant, but I recognized her very well."

"Were they arguing? Angry?"

"Not at all. Laughing. Smiling. Talking. Who is the guy?"

"New man in town. Never mind about that. Can you tell me: did anything unusual happen? Interesting?"

"Not a thing. They seemed to be having a wonderful time. Left before we did."

Toby wanted to gnash his teeth. He'd never found out where Rickward was staying either. Could be both Rickward and Sharlene were staying at the same place.

"Caro saw her last night at Apple Blossoms eating with a man. I think it was Gordon Rickward."

Detective Eddie's brow lifted. "The same guy who bailed Aaron Evanston."

"Amy met him at Apple Blossoms last night. I'm going to call the bed and breakfast and see if he's staying there."

"Hold on. Let's let dispatch do it. Maisie'll be more apt to pass along information."

Nodding, Toby listened while the detective made the call. Ten minutes later, dispatch was on the radio talking with Detective Eddie again. When he finished, he headed toward his vehicle. "If you're coming with me, you'd better hop to it."

Toby didn't ask questions.

Detective put his siren on, and they sped two miles out of town. When he pulled up to the bed and breakfast, both men opened their doors together. Toby ran for the front door, not waiting on Detective Eddie or his permission.

"What room is Rickward in?" Toby yelled the question as he plowed into the front desk.

"I'm sorry—" Maisie, the owner, was being disagreeable as usual.

"We just want to talk with him, Maisie." Detective Eddie stepped up beside Toby.

"Since it's you, Detective Eddie, I guess it will be all right. Try to keep it as quiet as possible." With no small amount of displeasure she handed over a key. "Can't you knock?"

"Yes, and we will at first."

The two didn't wait for any more comments from the owner, but sprinted up the stairs.

A knock on the door didn't elicit a response. Detective Eddie knocked again and called out. "Rickward, we need to talk with you a moment."

No answer.

Detective Eddie inserted the key and shoved the door open.

On the bed lay Amy, her eyes closed.

"Amy." Toby rushed over to her. "Are you okay?"

Her eyes flickered open, and a smile spread her lips. "Of course, I'm okay. Untie me, please."

"Who did this to you, Little Amy?" Detective Eddie's face was as stern as Toby had ever seen it.

Her gaze switched to Toby who was rubbing her wrists. "Gordon Rickward."

Anger exploded through Toby. "Why would he do this? You're not hurt? Are you sure?"

"I'm fine. He wanted me to tell him where it was."

"Where what was?"

"I have no clue. He didn't even know. He acted a little crazy."

"Tell us what happened." Detective Eddie pulled up a chair close to the side of the bed.

"Nothing to tell. We had dinner. He escorted me home. Said good-bye, and the next thing I knew, I woke up in here. I knew right away I wasn't in a dungeon." She grinned. "I figured it was some kind of hotel or private room in a house. But I had no clue it was Gordon until he walked in."

"Why would he do that? Do you think he didn't realize you could identify him?"

Toby exchanged a glance with Detective Eddie. Maybe Gordon wasn't worried. After he got his information, maybe...

Later, after Detective Eddie called for his officer to come and process the place, he dropped them both off at her home. They stood watching as his car left.

"I was really scared, Amy."

"I wasn't."

"You weren't?"

"I knew you'd come."

Chapter Twenty-one

Monday afternoon, Toby dialed a number. "Detective Eddie, can you meet me here at Undiscovered Treasures? And bring Mr. Cowell and his grandson?"

"Why?"

"Want to reveal what I've learned and see their reactions."

"Might be a good time for me to do a little of that revealing. I've got some new information.

The smugness in Appleton's policeman was enough to rouse Toby's curiosity. "Six?"

"Six it is. Provided we can get those two there."

"They're coming?" Amy blurted out her anxious question before Toby could hang up.

"Yep."

"Toby, do you really think they'll tell us anything?" Excitement blazed from Amy's eyes.

"Maybe. Maybe not. But you can't argue with facts."

"True. But that doesn't make them guilty."

"They may not be. I'm not expecting a confession."

"What about Gordon?"

"From what Detective Eddie said, he must have skipped town."

"Really?"

"Along with a certain attorney."

Amy's frowned. "Who?"

"Sharlene Miller."

"I'm not surprised. We suspected they were

an item."

"I imagine our chief has put out an alert for them, to bring charges against him for kidnapping you. And I have my suspicions she's not entirely on the up and up." Toby sank onto the stool behind the countertop. "I'm wondering what else our police chief has up his sleeve."

Amy was staring out the front window. "I think we're about to find out."

~*~

Detective Eddie was the first to arrive at Undiscovered Treasures, with Barnabas Cowell and Aaron Evanston arriving ten minutes later.

On their heels, Jazzi ran into the shop and huffed an apology. "Hope it's okay that I came."

Toby nodded at her even as he took in Amy's hug and smile for her sister. Whatever had happened between them the night Aaron had scared Jazzi so much, it had bonded them tight. By the looks of it, they weren't only sisters now, but good friends too. He switched his gaze to the chief. "Detective Eddie, do you want to go first?"

"Sure." The man stood and took a couple steps forward. "Here's what we know. First, Mr. Cowell, your oldest son was killed while serving a term as a state senator. Your oldest daughter was accused, but never convicted, of a Ponzi scheme. Neither of these had a child. That left your youngest. You and your daughter had a falling out when she refused to listen to your reasoning and married a man you considered unsuitable for her.

"Her husband had a son from a previous marriage who was just smart enough to work his way to the top of his business choice. You could have accepted him, I figure, but he had a problem with money. He was—is—a spender and never seemed to be able to save. That was a big turn off for you.

"Fortunately, your daughter and husband had a child together. Aaron Evanston. You seldom saw him—sometimes years at a time before they favored you with a visit. The way we hear it, you would have taken either one of these children into your care, but your daughter wouldn't allow it.

"How am I doing?"

Cowell gave him a sour look and didn't speak.

"Nevertheless, you kept tabs on both Gordon Rickward and Aaron through your lawyers and the PIs you hired to find out whatever you wanted to know. By the way, we know Gordon changed his last name to his mother's maiden name. You realized, even after several encouraging talks with Gordon, that his spending habits would never change, yet you gave him one more opportunity, didn't you? When he came to you for money to pay a gambling debt, you didn't refuse him, but paid it off with the warning that unless he curbed his ways, he'd see no more money from you."

"How did you learn all that? It's not common knowledge." The old man scowled at the chief.

"But when you dig deep enough, you can find out just about anything. Gordon Rickward, in spite of being quite the man in his circles, couldn't keep his actions from the news. It was easy enough from there to find who covered his debts. Who else in his limited family members could do that for him? He didn't know how lucky he was to have a man who was willing to accept him as a grandchild, if he would have only learned."

For the first time, sadness creased the old man's face. One hand lifted and scrubbed across his features, then his body straightened. "You might as well continue. I doubt you'll quit now."

"Just a bit more about Rickward. I'm assuming now, that the man—out of favor with you—overheard or found out in another way, some information about a hidden valuable item you'd been searching for. Isn't that why you visited Toby's shop? Was he and Aaron in cahoots together? Did Rickward put Aaron up to breaking in at Undiscovered Treasures and Bloomin' Life or was it you who put Rickward up to it?"

For a long moment, Mr. Cowell sat with bowed head. But Toby guessed the reason was more to figure how to proceed, what to tell and what to leave out, than sadness at his family's misdeeds.

"No. I suspect Gordon overheard a topic being discussed and tried to find out what the item was and where. Aaron had nothing to do with any of this."

"So you keep saying. But his actions are not those of an innocent man. As of right now, my officer is searching your house for evidence."

"I didn't give you that permission. You need a search warrant." The old man was beside himself with rage.

"And right here it is." Detective Eddie handed it over.

"I'll be calling my lawyer." Mr. Cowell threatened.

"Sharlene Miller? Yes, my contacts in Charleston was able to find that bit of information too. By the way, do you have a new one? I'm afraid she's skipped town, and there's a warrant for her companion's arrest going out across the tri-state area."

"Gordon might be a scoundrel, but she's done nothing wrong. And neither has Aaron."

"Are you sure about that?" Toby interjected the question. That man who'd run across the rooftop could very well have been Aaron."

Aaron sat on his chair, bent over, and appeared to be totally unconnected to the conversation.

Old man Cowell cast a glance at Aaron, then spoke again. "I'm sure. Aaron's not always been the most well behaved young man, especially with a role model such as his father, but he understands now he needs to mend his ways or he'll not see a penny of my money. He's given his word he'll be on his best behavior from here on out."

"Well, we should know shortly. We have a witness who can describe the man's shoes."

Mr. Cowell could do nothing but shake his head.

"And what is this item you've been searching for? Why would you need to search for it?" Detective Eddie's hand went to his mustache.

The old man shook his head. "That I can't answer. It's why I wanted all those pieces of furniture from you, Gibson, and from your lady friend at the auction. I've been searching for years—"

It was time to bring out the piece of information Toby had found online. "It wouldn't be the item your great-great-grandfather stole with his fellow sailors back in the mid-eighteen hundreds, would it?"

"How did you find that out? I squashed that bit of gossip that resurfaced years ago." Cowell's face had turned a bright red.

"As our detective has already said, if you dig deep enough, you can find just about anything."

"So it would seem."

"The article said all the sailors except your ancestor died a terrible death in the ship's fire."

"So I've heard."

"Sounds kind of fishy to me. No pun intended."

"I wasn't there so I can't speculate on how my great-great-grandfather escaped."

"I bet." Toby couldn't keep the sarcasm from his voice. "What was so strange, was the article linked to that one. It said in Spain, several million dollars—according to today's estimate—were stolen right about the time your ancestor set sail from there."

"Now that is odd, but no proof." Mr. Cowell stood. "If you're done talking hearsay, I have business to attend to."

"One last question." Detective Eddie put out a hand to stop Cowell. "Why were you searching at auctions? You had to have had a reason."

The longest sigh Toby had ever heard blew from Cowell's mouth. "Gordon misunderstood my instructions and cleaned out a room filled with antique furniture, putting it up for auction. I never liked the stuff—it was homemade, thus the confusion. I suspect Gordon eavesdropped on my and Aaron's conversation and realized what a mistake he'd made. If the treasure was in any of that furniture, he'd buy it back himself and search it. If he could find the treasure, he'd be set for life. I can't confirm that accusation, but I suspect it to be true."

"But if you thought it might be hidden in that furniture, why hadn't you already searched it? And why had you never stayed at this property before?"

"That sounds like three questions to me," growled the man.

"I'd like an answer." Detective Eddie wasn't going to be put off.

"This property here in West Virginia has been in our family from way back. As far as I know, none of the family stayed here much. Didn't care for the area, so I assumed anything of value wouldn't be hidden here. As a last resort, I decided to move here—at least temporarily—and do some diligent searching. Once some of the furniture was sold—mistakenly—and then Gordon showed up again—I'd ordered him to leave—it threw us off kilter. Does that answer all your questions?"

Detective Eddie held up a hand as he answered his radio. "What did you find?"

He listened a moment, then turned back to Mr. Cowell and Aaron. "Aaron, I'm arresting you on the charge of breaking and entering, at the least. More charges might be forthcoming shortly."

"Mr. Cowell, you can go for now." Detective

Eddie waved him away. "Don't leave town."

"Are you really going to keep Mr. Cowell here in town, Detective Eddie?" Amy walked over to the man, but continued to stare after the old man who seemed to have aged another decade as he left the room.

"For a month or so. Just in case. Not about to go traipsing all over the country looking for him."

"What did your officer find?" Toby asked.

"Shoes that match your description. A few items that we suspect came from Caro's treasure chest, and a filthy shirt that was covered in dirt."

"Looks like Aaron's guilty." Toby agreed.

"Maybe. I have a feeling Rickward was behind Aaron's acts. I'm thinking he was either blackmailing him or luring him to do the dirty work, making him think they would strike it rich and share alike."

"I doubt that would have happened." Toby couldn't see that man sharing anything.

"Aaron wanted me to go back with him." The sadness—or was it plain melancholy?—in Jazzi's voice was mixed with determination.

"Jazzi. You're not going to, are you? If he was rough with you once, he will do so again." Amy slipped an arm around her sister.

"No. I've had my fill of him. I can't trust him, and if there's one thing I hate, it's a man that can't be trusted. No matter what his grandfather says, he's not changed." Jazzi circled her arm around Amy's back. "Thank you for loving me even when I was unlovable. Wish Mom and Dad were here so I could tell them."

"They'll know, don't doubt it for a minute. Besides, they'll slip in soon, and you can tell them as many times as you want till they take off again."

"I do have a confession to make though." Jazzi's fingers twisted together.

"What is it?" Anxiousness shone from Amy's eyes.

The girl took a deep breath. "Toby..."

"You don't have to tell me. I know, Jazzi."

"You do? How?"

"Yes. It took me awhile to figure it out, but you and Aaron stole a few of those trinkets off the shelf, didn't you?"

"Yes. I'm so sorry. Until I came back and saw what a steady, great life Amy was living, I thought it was all fun and games to live as I wanted. Stealing and being plain wild. I'm sorry. I'll pay you back."

"It was your perfume. When I came in one night it triggered a memory, but I couldn't place it for a long time."

Toby watched the two sisters walking away. Hopefully, Jazzi had learned her lesson and would change her ways. With Amy to guide her, maybe the adjustment would be an easy one for her. How could anyone go wrong with someone like Amy beside them? She was the sweetest person on earth. He had never appreciated her enough, and it was about time he started to do so.

"What's next? Are we finished with this?" Toby turned to Detective Eddie.

"Don't see how we have much else to go on. If the old man with all his resources can't find his own treasure, don't see how we can. When we find Rickward, we'll get him for kidnapping, but until then, I think we're done."

"I didn't think of this until after I remembered Jazzi's perfume, but everytime someone broke into my shop, I smelled a cologne I didn't recognize. It was only when Amy and I recognized a man's cologne in Starli's office the night of Andy and Caro's welcome home party that it clicked. I thought at first it was Aaron who might have stolen her key to get into her shop easier, but realize now it had to have been Rickward. He's the one who kept breaking into my shop.

"You think so?"

"I know so. But I do think he sent Aaron to Amy's—too dirty of a job for Rickward—and also into the empty building between our shops to spy on me."

"Makes sense. We'll take your statement and Amy's too, tomorrow."

"That sounds like a plan to me. I'd just as soon never see Rickward again but if it helps put him behind bars, then I'm for it. I'm going to have to do some extra praying to forgive him for the way he handled Amy. He didn't steal anything at my shop, but not for lack of trying. But he made a nuisance of himself and disturbed my sleep."

"And who knows what else we'll come up with?" Detective Eddie stretched.

"Will we see you at opening night of the play?"

"With get-in-free tickets? You bet. Break a leg, kiddo."

Toby chuckled to himself. Detective Eddie might never consider Toby a real adult. But Toby liked the man anyway.

Chapter Twenty-two

Amy was peeking between the curtains when Toby strode up to her to take a look.

"It's packed."

"Did you think it wouldn't be?" Amy teased. "That everyone would stay away because of a change in actors at the last minute?"

"Well..."

"I made sure they didn't." Ryle was right behind them. "And I've got your backs tonight. Just calm down, Toby, and take a deep breath. We'll cue you if you forget your lines."

He had to be teasing. Toby knew the play from front to back.

"And with Amy's acting, how can he go wrong? She's a pro." Caro walked up and took her own peek through the curtains.

"Am I to understand you don't think I'm a pro?" Toby put on a grieved air.

"You'll do all right, brother. Don't get your dander stirred." Caro patted his shoulder, then jerked back to avoid the playful smack he aimed at her.

"Some support." Toby's pout was so overdone, the rest laughed.

"Take your places, people." Ryle spoke in a quiet, but commanding voice.

Amy led Toby to his place and whirled to stand in front of him. "We'll be fine. We've got this, Tobias Lee Gibson."

Carole Brown

And with those simple words, his nervousness vanished.

~*~

They were entering into the last scene with a short five minute break. Toby took the bottle of water from Ryle and swallowed half of it. By the sound of the audience's enthusiastic responses, this newest play of Caro's was a success. The donation to a local charity should be huge.

"You guys are doing great." Ryle beamed at both of them. "I'm glad I talked you into it. Much better than Krissy or Jason could have pulled off. And Amy—I've never seen anyone do as well. The audience loves her. I'll be surprised if she doesn't have fellows lined up at her door proposing."

Toby bit his lip to keep from speaking the retort he wanted to make. "She is good."

"Good? Are you crazy? She's fantastic. You'd be making a serious mistake not to coax her to act in all your plays. She's the perfect sweetheart."

You can't have her. I won't let you. She's mine.

Where had those words come from? But Toby knew. Straight from his heart.

"Take your places." Ryle had walked away and now raised his voice.

Toby's heart was beating so fast he wondered if he'd be able to even say his first lines. The scene was a short one, but the most important one of the play.

The curtains opened.

"I've made my choice." Amy's stage voice was clear, showing a bit of diffidence and determination. "I'm going to live with Aunt Lizzie in Charleston. I'll have a much better chance of getting a good teaching job there."

"You can't go." Toby's reply was both a plea and command.

"I can't keep the farm. You know that. It's the sensible thing to do. I have no other choice."

Toby looked up as if gazing at the stars, thinking. "You have one other choice, the way I see it."

"Whatever do you mean? I—"

Toby turned, looked at her, then strode purposely toward her. He took her hand and stared into her eyes. "You do indeed have another choice. And I'm going to give it to you."

He dropped to one knee, still holding her hand. "I can't let you go, My Love. I can't live without you. You mean the world to me, and I've been a cad to not admit it. Everyone around me knew, and my heart knew, but I refused the knowledge. But no longer."

"Toby. What are you saying?"

Her tremulous voice was so quiet, Toby wondered if anyone but him had heard her question.

But he forgot about the audience listening with bated breath. He forgot about his sister and best friend, Andy, and even about Ryle. The only thing he could think of at the moment was her answer. Had he put it off too long? Taken advantage of her friendship till the love had simmered dry?

No. It couldn't be. He wouldn't allow it. With all the persuasion he could possibly put into the question, he did so now. "Will you marry me? Amy, will you be my wife? Be mine, please."

Too late, he realized he'd said Amy's name instead of her stage name, but he didn't care. His mind was closed to any thoughts but what her answer would be. Would she spite him with a refusal? Laugh at his clumsy attempt of a proposal at the worst of times?

"Toby, do you mean it? Are you serious?"

He gazed up into her blue-green eyes that appeared as shining stars filled with tears. Toby stood and gathered her close. "I've never been more serious in my life. I love you."

As his declaration rang out strong and clear throughout the auditorium, the audience stood to their feet, cheering and clapping. No one but him heard her whispered words in his ear.

"Yes, Toby, I will. Forever and forever."

Chapter Twenty-three

One month later

The first of June, Toby and Amy said their "I dos" in front of family and friends in the Appleton Park. Amy had insisted she wanted no big wedding to-do, but a simple one with those they loved close by, and Toby had gone along with her wishes.

He'd endured enough teasing, over his public declaration of love to Amy during the play, to last him a life-time. He was glad getting the wedding plans in order had taken precedence. And now as they sat together at the reception, she handed him an envelope.

"This is my wedding gift to you." Her eyes twinkled their usual green and blue shards of color at him. "Open it."

He did, and drew out a bundle of papers, but it was the top one that he read. When he finished he looked at her. "You bought this for me?"

"Well, not exactly. Once you proposed, I figured we'd better both own that piece of property between our businesses. As soon as you sign it, it will be ours. Or at least ours to pay for..."

"But my agent said it was sold to another buyer."

"I spoke with him and told him my plans. Since he knows both of us, he agreed to allow you to think I bought it."

"And you hired Toni to remodel the inside?"

"Of course. Who else could do it as well? And it's finished except for one thing."

"What's that?"

"Oh, you'll find out tomorrow for your birthday."

"Is that why you said we didn't need a honeymoon right now?"

"Of course. Do you think Caro would forgive me if we missed it for a silly honeymoon?"

Her laughter was heavenly music.

"I see I'm going to have to keep my eye on you."

"I should hope you'll have eyes only for me. I'm going to be very jealous of your attention."

Her answer was pure cheek, and Toby loved it.

~*~

The next morning, Amy led Toby upstairs in the building they'd bought. "Close your eyes, Mr. Gibson. Your other birthday present is in this room. Don't look until I tell you to."

The way she was springing surprises at him, he wondered what was coming. He hadn't thought anything could top his birthday present with the donation from the K5 run going to his two favorite charities. If Amy kept this up, he'd be spoiled.

Felt pretty good to be loved so much.

"It won't bite, will it? You didn't go and get a dog, did you?"

"No. A wolf, Silly. Keep your eyes shut." She led him across the room and turned. "Now you can look."

It was just as he'd planned it months ago

when he'd tried to buy that monstrous homemade bedroom set at the auction where Amy had outbid him. The only thing needed was to put the bed together.

"Why didn't you have the guys put the bed up?"

She knelt and picked up one leg, only to have it tilt in her hands. "Had to leave something for you to do."

"Save the hardest for me, huh?"

"For us. I wanted to help you do our last piece of furniture for our bedroom." She lifted another leg and frowned. "No wonder these things are so heavy-duty. They are thick and *heavy*. I doubt they'll ever wear out."

"They certainly look untouched by time. Wonder what's the story behind them? Whoever did the work did a fantastic job. Old man Cowell may not have liked them much, but I think they're perfect. Thank you, Amy."

She didn't answer, only jumped up to retrieve a screwdriver and proceeded to dig at one of the legs. "Look, Toby, at the bottom of this leg. Doesn't it look funny?"

He leaned over to stare at what she was digging. "Don't damage it please."

"I won't. Just look."

"Let me see that." He pulled the leg to himself and took the screwdriver from her. With several strong probes, a three-inch piece of wood fell to floor and after it came a shower of gold coins tumbling like a waterfall.

"Toby." Amy whispered his name. "Is that...?"

He looked at her. "I think you're right. Hand me another leg."

One after another, each of the four legs

yielded a harvest of ancient coins.

Amy scooted close beside him, and they sat staring at the glimmering treasure.

"We found it. I can't believe this." Toby pulled her close and gave her a huge hug. "After all these years, Cowell and who knows who else of his ancestors who searched for them, we've got them right here in our soon-to-be home."

"What are we going to do about it?" Amy's voice was still in whisper mode.

"We could keep it."

"Just think what all we could buy."

"Yeah, we could. Or we could hide it again and will it to our children."

"Yes...but how do we feel about that?"

"Uncomfortable?"

"That, and wrong." Amy sighed. "If only we weren't so...so...so conscientious."

"But we are, and we want to be. So what's our other choices?"

"Do we have to give it back to Mr. Cowell?"

"I'd rather give it to charity."

"But I think we're going to have to call Detective Eddie and allow him to find who it really belongs to. If Cowell's great-great-grandfather and his cohorts did steal it, then it rightfully belongs to the country or business it was stolen from."

Why did Amy have to be so right? But he loved her honest little heart. "You're right, Beautiful, and I agree. Besides..."

"Besides what?"

"Besides, I have all the treasure I'll ever want right here within my arms."

"Me?"

"You."

And Toby proceeded to show her how much he treasured her with the kiss he laid on her lips.

The End.

Carole Brown

The Golden Touch

An Appleton, WV Romantic Mystery

Chapter One

Ryle Sadler stared at the unkept bed and breakfast in front of him. The urge to buy this place was stronger than ever, and he couldn't understand it. He'd never bought or invested in anything on an urge. He'd prayed about it for sure. Many times. No answer came back from God. Only this confusing urge to buy it. Now.

He hadn't amassed his wealth by going on urges. No sirree. Coming from the poor side of town had taught him plenty, and two of those things were listening and learning. Those had gotten him where he was now.

The Golden Touch. That's what the investors in the world called it, and that's what he had. Or so they said. It scared him, truth be told, that everything he touched turned to gold. Didn't matter whether it was stocks or an act of generosity in helping a struggling business person. Every time—so far—had been successful.

But this, this business that Maisie, the owner, cared little about, was neither of those things. If he bought it, would it change his touch? Would it be his first failure? After all, what did he know about bed and breakfasts?

Nothing.

A young woman exited the place, her purple hair a distraction from her beautiful features. Jazzi Sanderson didn't know her own beauty

1

or worth.

He'd had little to do with women. Too little time, and, frankly, no one so far, who'd garnered his attention long enough.

But this woman. Ryle's heart gave an unusual ping forcing a frown on his face.

She saw him then, and gave a shy, little wave, the smile on her face as bright as the sunshine from the heavens.

And then he heard the voice.

Invite Jazzi Sanderson to help you at the bed and breakfast.

No. That was crazy. What was wrong with him? He'd never done such a thing. Invested in businesses by using his money, yes, to do what he felt was his calling. But asking a woman he barely knew to help him get this place up and running? Would she laugh at him? Would the whole town of Appleton consider him the biggest fool ever to cross their path?

She did have a reputation. And not such a good one.

What if she accepted, thinking it was a lark—an easy way to get some money—with no improvement in her personality? But was that his responsibility?

No. But then, he didn't think helping someone continue on the broken path they were on was beneficial either. Still, his calling was to help. What they did afterwards was their responsibility.

So, what's it to be? Will you obey my direction on this?

The dark cloud suddenly covering the sun

seemed to be frowning at him.

"I always have." Ryle couldn't even hear his own whisper as he mouthed the words.

And as suddenly, as it had been covered seconds ago, the sun popped from behind the cloud, sending its golden beams straight down to shine on the bed and breakfast.

Ryle gave up the struggle. It might be interesting—and a learning process for him—if this adventure was a failure. Time would tell.

The groan that escaped his lips assured him he wasn't looking forward to it.

Books by Carole Brown

Women's Fiction:
The Redemption of Caralynne Haymen

Misc
West Virginia Scrapbook

Denton and Alex Davies Mysteries:
Hog Insane
Bat Crazy

Spies of World War II
With Music In Their Hearts
A Flute in the Willows

The Appleton Mysteries
Sabotaged Christmas
Knight in Shining Apron
Undiscovered Treasures
Toby's Troubles

Award winning author Carole Brown loves to weave suspense and tough topics into her books, along with a touch of romance and whimsy.

She is always on the lookout for outstanding titles and catchy ideas.

Carole and Dan, her pastor husband, reside in SE Ohio and have ministered and counseled across the country. Together, they enjoy their grandsons, traveling, gardening, good food, the simple life, and did she mention their grandsons?

Carole loves to connect with her readers. You can find her at her blog:
Sunnebnkwrtr.blogspot.com/
And facebook:
www.facebook.com/CaroleBrown.author

If you enjoyed reading this book, let others know... and bless Carole Brown with an honest review.

Made in the USA
Columbia, SC
11 July 2018